Taking the Bull by the Horns

MJ Fredrick

Chapter One

"Aaron!"

The dark-haired imp broke from the herd of kindergartners and bolted. Lavender Prouty pushed her straight blonde hair out of her face and pivoted in pursuit. Controlling her class at the Cascade rodeo arena was like herding cats. The children wanted to see every animal at once, and Aaron was determined to see the cows.

The extra fifteen pounds Lavender had put on since her grandmother joined Pinterest slowed her down—not that she'd ever been a match for a five-year-old. Aaron would be through the bars and astride a cow before she caught him.

A lean figure stepped between Aaron and the cow pen. Strong arms snatched him up, swinging him in midair so his squeal echoed off the metal roof of the barn. The cowboy tucked the boy under his arm and turned toward her, grey eyes twinkling beneath the brim of a straw hat.

"Nice moves. You could teach a quarter horse a thing or two," he told the boy, then turned to Lavender. "This belong to you?"

His deep voice sent a shiver of female awareness down her

spine. Low voices were definitely a weakness. But he moved closer, and his shoulder length brown hair swung back to reveal a young face. Of course, lots of the cowboys who came to town for the Cascade Rodeo were young. Why was she surprised? Worse, why was she disappointed?

She reached for Aaron and her bare arm slid along the cowboy's. His warm skin against her sensitive inner wrist almost caused her to snatch her hand away before she had a secure hold on the kindergartner. She anchored Aaron in front of her, both hands on his shoulders, and looked up at the cowboy.

"He's for sale. Cheap."

The boy squirmed.

"Maybe we'll get this nice cowboy to hogtie you," she chided. "How's that?"

"Be happy to." The cowboy played along, the corner of his mouth hitched up as he drew a length of rope from the back pocket of his worn Levis.

She loved Levis almost as much as she loved deep voices.

Aaron burrowed against her thighs—right, like she wanted the cowboy's attention *there*—as he cowered from the rope. Lavender crouched before him and gave him her sternest look, which, granted, wasn't all that stern. "The next time you get away from me or Mrs. Mainka, I'll let him do it. Now go on back with the class." She set him in the direction of the rest of the class and her room mother.

The cowboy with the laughing eyes hadn't moved away. In her desire to be clever, she'd neglected to thank him.

"Thank you," she remedied now, a little breathless that he was so close.

"I'd rather herd cows than kids." He stepped beside her to watch her class, who were envying some pigs their wallow in the mud. Mrs. Mainka was doing an admirable job of keeping the children from joining the swine and guilt tugged at Lavender for not giving her a hand. But the cowboy hadn't wandered off and she wasn't sure how to take her leave of him.

Or if she was ready to.

"Mm, yeah, kids have a way of figuring things out that cows never would."

He folded tanned muscular arms over his chest, drawing her attention to his half-buttoned shirt and smooth flat pecs. She curled her hand into a fist, surprised by the urge to touch. She hadn't allowed herself an urge in – well, it was depressing to think about.

"Do you work here?" she asked to distract herself. Was that even the proper terminology?

His smile was lopsided, his teeth straight and white. "I'm here for the rodeo," he acknowledged. "I'm Taylor Craig."

He held out his hand, and looked at her like he expected that name to mean something. She merely slipped her hand into his. It was less squeeze than caress, his thumb riding over the back of her hand, his touch lingering as if he could learn something from the shape of her hand before sliding away, along her palm. All the while, those grey eyes focused on her. She'd read Victorian novels about women wearing gloves to avoid intimate contact with a man's hand and had dismissed the idea as repressed. But now... Heat crept up her throat and her pale skin would advertise her reaction. She turned quickly back to her class but still couldn't walk away. What was wrong with her?

"Lavender Prouty," she murmured.

"Lavender? Unusual."

"Yeah, that was my parents. Unusual."

He still didn't move away, and now she was nervous. What did he want, exactly?

"Do you ride?" She hadn't made conversation with a cowboy before, had never wanted to. Heck, she hadn't been to the rodeo in years, though it opened every weekend. "I mean, what event?"

His smile went back to half-mast, almost self-deprecating. "Steer wrestling, this week."

She flicked her gaze to his. He had such gorgeous eyes. She dragged her thoughts back to the rodeo. Did cowboys ride in more than one event? Didn't they specialize? "This week?"

He lifted a shoulder. "Yeah, well, last season I tried calf roping, this year team roping. Not my sport."

"You still have the rope." She nodded to the length he ran through his hands.

"Yeah, well, I don't like anything to beat me, you know? I still practice."

She perked up. Rarely had she met a man who admitted a weakness, especially a man this good-looking.

How long would he be able to keep those pretty teeth in the rodeo?

"So you like steer wrestling?" She considered his lean, muscular form. Those steer probably outweighed him three or four times. Heck, she probably outweighed him.

"Pretty well."

"Are you any good?"

"I have decent timing."

What did that mean? From the glint in his eyes, she got that he meant it to be a double entendre. She stepped back, unaccustomed to the unwavering attention of a handsome man.

Handsome boy. He had to be in his early twenties, and she was thirty-four. So why was he looking at her like he wanted to eat her up? Her blonde hair was flying every which way and she was wearing a boxy red T-shirt with the school's bucking bronco logo. Admittedly her new jeans were cute, but that wasn't enough to spark the look in his eyes.

"My kids are getting away from me," she said breathlessly,

backing away, unable to believe she'd left twenty five-year-olds with her room mother while she flirted. She'd never done anything so irresponsible on the job. Or otherwise.

He followed her slowly, both hands in his front pockets, clearly reveling in her nervousness. "Would they like to come meet my horse?"

They'd moved too close to her class when he said it, and the children overheard.

"We want to see the horse!"

"I love horses!"

"Miss Prouty, we want to see his horse." This last was emphasized with a tug at the hem of her T-shirt.

Yeah, she was great with the discipline.

"Honestly, these are ranch kids for the most part," she grumbled at him. "You'd think they'd never seen animals before. I thank you for your offer, but—"

"Oh, but my horse is special." He turned his charm on her class when she edged away.

Okay, let him try. Other than that whole Santa Claus/Tooth Fairy thing, five-year-olds didn't swallow BS easily.

Back in the safety of his comrades, Aaron issued the challenge with a lift of his chin. "Nuh-uh."

Taylor Craig matched his stance, eyes alight with humor. "My horse is the smartest horse in the world."

"No, it's not," Aaron retorted, and was echoed by his companions.

Taylor stretched out a hand. "I'll bet you a dollar she is."

"Deal." Aaron thrust his hand upward and Taylor shook solemnly.

Okay, low voices, Levis, and guys who liked kids and animals. Those were her weaknesses when it came to men. Lavender tore her gaze away as Taylor straightened and looked at her.

"Let's go, then." He ambled ahead of the class, who followed, no herding needed.

Lavender exchanged a glance with Mrs. Mainka, who no doubt saw more than Lavender wanted her to, and they trailed behind the children.

Taylor shuffled to a halt in the stables in front of a breath-taking Palomino mare with a long silky mane and a wide white blaze.

"She's beautiful," Lavender said, stepping in front of her class, focused on the horse.

"I have a thing for blondes," Taylor said.

The teasing lilt in his voice drew her attention and he winked at her. She blushed and turned away. Why was he flirting with her? Or was she misreading? It had been a long time since someone had flirted with her. "What's her name?"

Taylor ran his hand down the side of the horse's neck. Lavender followed the path with her gaze, the long, strong fingers soothing on the mare's throat. Lavender swallowed, feeling the caress on her own skin. The mare tossed her head, shaking out her mane.

"Angelina." He reached over the stall door to hook a rope on the horse's bridle before he opened the door to lead her out onto the packed dirt aisle.

Mrs. Mainka guided the children along the stalls on the opposite side of the aisle, out of the way.

"She won't step on them," Taylor said. "She likes kids."

"She's not used to twenty at once. Sometimes *I* step on them."

He chuckled. "You want to see her trick?" he asked the children.

"Yes!" The chorus echoed off the metal roof.

To her credit, Angelina only swiveled her ears, but didn't

flinch at the noise. Lavender met Taylor's eyes and smiled. He grinned back, then turned to her class.

"I need a volunteer." Without waiting for hands, he pointed to Esmi, one of Lavender's favorites, a quiet girl with a long dark braid, glasses and a serious round face. "Here, honey, you want to give me a hand?"

Apparently his charm didn't translate to five-year-old girls, because Esmi shrank away shyly. All the other students waved their hands wildly but Taylor wouldn't take no for an answer.

"Do you like horses, honey?"

Esmi shook her head and cowered against Lavender's thigh. She rested her hand on Esmi's shoulder.

"Esmi loves horses. Don't you?" she urged the child.

"Esmi," Taylor repeated. "I know she's big." He glanced over his shoulder at Angelina, whose ears pricked forward, her focus on Taylor. "But she's the sweetest horse you'll ever meet. She'd never hurt you. All you have to do is stand. She'll do all the work. You want to try?" He held out a hand, his elbow resting on his knee, fingers tilted toward her, offering but not persuasive, so patient, reading the child so well.

Esmi put her hand in his. He straightened with a grin and led her to the horse. Angelina lowered her big head to inspect the girl curiously and Esmi scrambled back, tucking her arms against her chest. Taylor curved his hand over her shoulder and urged her forward for Angelina's inspection. Angelina widened her nostrils, then lifted her head. Esmi shuddered but held her ground. Taylor waited a moment to ensure she'd stay put, then walked the few steps to Angelina's head.

"Okay, I'm going to ask Angelina if you're a boy or a girl. She'll paw the ground twice if you're a girl and once if you're a boy. Got it?"

"Got it!" the class chorused.

Taylor released Angelina to rejoin Esmi. "Okay, Angelina. Is Esmi a boy or girl?"

Angelina lifted her front hoof and struck the packed earth twice. The children oohed. Esmi grinned and melted back into the class. Taylor beckoned to a boy, Michael, who took Esmi's place, his finger in his mouth. So Taylor was good at noticing the shy ones. Lavender tried not to be impressed.

Angelina repeated her trick accurately four times before the class grew restless, attention wandering.

So Taylor crooked a finger at Lavender. She picked her way through the class, wary of his intention. He wrapped his fingers around her upper arm. She winced in embarrassment as his fingers sank into the softness of her flesh. Like he couldn't tell from looking that she was a little on the fluffy side.

"Okay, Angelina," he said when he had Lavender positioned where he wanted her. "Boy or girl?"

Angelina lifted her head and whinnied. The children screeched and covered their ears, like they weren't louder.

Taylor laughed. "See? She said, 'Woman.'"

Lavender laughed, too. It had indeed sounded like Angelina had said "Woman." How often did he use that trick to pick up girls?

She patted the side of Angelina's neck. "Okay, children, we need to let Mr. Craig get back to whatever he needs to do to get ready for the rodeo. Tell him thank you."

The children did, then she did, quietly, not meeting his gaze, though she wanted to. He didn't move when she walked away— she was very aware of that—but didn't look back to see if he was watching her.

"Miss Prouty."

Now she had to turn back or appear rude.

"I hear Busbee's barbecue is pretty good. Any truth to that?"

She smiled. "Not that there are a lot of choices around here, but yeah, it's pretty good."

"So what time is school out?" He nodded toward her retreating class.

"What?" He couldn't be asking...could he? She certainly couldn't answer the way she wanted.

He took a step toward her, letting out the lead rope so Angelina stayed back, his gaze intent on her. "I don't like to eat alone."

She just bet he didn't. He probably never had to. Except tonight.

"Thanks for being so good to my kids." She backed away, though every nerve in her screamed to say yes. Her brain chided those eager hormones. *He'll just leave you like everyone else. Is it worth it?* To which her hormones, looking at his hands and his mouth screamed, *Yes!* But as always, Lavender listened to her brain. Easier not to get hurt that way. She turned from Taylor. "Good luck to you and Angelina."

"Miss Prouty, I'm asking you out to dinner," he said, still pursuing.

Her face heated. Why her? She pushed back her hair self-consciously. He was handsome, and younger than her, enough that he was no doubt aware of it. And with her round face and ass, her straw-straight hair, well, she couldn't be his regular type. God knew he wasn't hers.

Even if he was, he'd be gone by Monday and she just didn't have the resources to be left again.

"Sorry, Mr. Craig."

The glint in his eyes dimmed at the regret in her tone. He touched the brim of his hat and turned away.

"Thanks again," she was compelled to call after him, then hurried after her class.

*****

Taylor pulled his F-150 into the school parking lot just before three. Apparently school had just let out because little kids milled in front of the building. And there on the steps, arms crossed over her red T-shirt, blonde hair whipping in her face, stood Lavender.

He could have found another dinner partner—the buckle bunnies had descended on the fairgrounds even though the rodeo was two days out. But Jesus, since he was fourteen, females had thrown themselves at him. For a time, he'd eaten it up like sugar. And like sugar it had grown old, though not fast enough. Still, the effect was long lasting, and now a woman who shied away, who blushed when he looked at her, captured his attention. He hadn't known women did that anymore.

Chasing a woman for a change would feel good. With Lavender, he'd have that chance. He pushed open the truck door and got out slowly, watching her. He'd liked how she was with her class, liked her sense of humor, liked her shy smile.

Look at that. She'd seen him and turned as red as her T-shirt. He grinned and straightened to his full height, tucking his hands in his pockets. She hurried down the steps and across the yard to the parking lot.

He reached into the truck, his movements languid, and plucked the little straw hat off the dashboard.

"What are you doing here?" she asked, very schoolteacher-ish, her posture stiff.

He held the hat out to her, his hand spanning the small crown. "Aaron left this." He turned the hat over to show her the boy's name on the sweatband.

Her shoulders relaxed and her eyes went soft. "Oh, thank goodness! He was ready to cry thinking he'd lost this." She took the hat and pressed it over her breasts like a shield. "You deliver lost and found items in your free time?"

"Just when I know where to find the owner." He glanced toward the school. "Or maybe not."

"He's going to appreciate this so much. I'll run out to his home to give it to him."

Surprise tugged his lips into a smile. "You deliver lost and found items in your free time?" he echoed.

She lowered her lashes. "He was really upset. You'll be his hero for bringing this back."

Taylor stepped back and yanked open the stiff driver's side door. "Then let me go with you to deliver it."

Her hesitation was appealing as hell, indecision clouding her eyes, the desire to agree, her battle against the desire. She looked over her shoulder at three other teachers standing on the school steps, watching her with open curiosity, and her shoulders stiffened again.

She turned back to him. "That would make Aaron very happy."

Taylor was fairly certain that wasn't her whole reason for agreeing. She started around the hood toward the passenger side door.

"That door doesn't open from the outside."

Her brows winged up in surprise, but she came back around and ducked under his arm to climb in. He slid in beside her. Nervously she fumbled with the buckle of the seat belt. He leaned over to take the buckle from her and clicked it home. His knuckles rested on her hip for a moment, just long enough for her to draw in a breath in awareness. He lifted his gaze to hers, saw the longing, the regret. Why was she so determined to keep him at a distance?

Why was he so determined to close it?

She swallowed and he eased back to start the truck. "Tell me where to go."

Chapter Two

The twenty minute drive over caliche roads passed in rapid-fire conversation that made Taylor feel like he'd been hit by a dust devil. Only a few questions got her talking, but mostly about her class. She talked a mile a minute about "her kids," and grew more animated, but the way she jittered in her seat and messed with her hair told him she hadn't really relaxed. Talking about her class was just another shield.

Still, he liked listening to her lightning-fast voice, the snap of her Texas accent. And while she was talking, he didn't have to talk about himself, or come up with a story about his past.

Following her directions, he pulled in front of a low ranch house that had seen better days. From the activity around the place—animals, bright plastic kid toys—he figured the neglect was based more on low priority than low funds. Behind the wooden fence, two kids smaller than Aaron raced around, and a pretty young woman stood watching the truck, her hands on her hips.

Taylor shoved at his door and it creaked open. Yeah, he could afford a better truck, but right now he needed to stay below the radar. Driving up to a small town rodeo in a brand new Dually would get him attention he didn't want, not yet.

He stepped out, aware of the young mother's eyes on him, and reached a hand in to Lavender. She paused, then took it, her hand small and soft, and she scooted across the vinyl seat, holding onto the hat.

He didn't let go of her hand when her feet hit the ground, instead rubbing his thumb over it, letting himself wonder what it would feel like on his body. She tugged it free and walked around the open door to the gate.

"Hey, Monica," Lavender said, her voice bright.

Monica smiled in return and opened the gate in welcome. "What are you doing out here, Lavender?"

"Taylor here found Aaron's hat." Lavender held the hat out and inclined her head in introduction.

Behind Monica, the screen door slammed and Aaron darted out, charging straight for his hat. He snatched it from Lavender with a whoop, and turned to Taylor, who'd come up beside her and leaned his forearms on the fence. Little eyes widened.

"Hey there, Mr. Craig. You want to see my pony?"

Taylor straightened. "Yeah, sure, if that's okay with your mom."

Monica lifted a shoulder, her cheeks dimpling, eyelashes lowering. "Sure. Aaron told me all about your horse, Mr. Craig. He's bound and determined to teach his pony some tricks now. Don't be too much of a pest, Aaron."

Lavender opened her mouth, then closed it again as Aaron grasped Taylor's hand and tugged him toward the barn.

Once the males had walked out of hearing range, Monica turned to Lavender with one eyebrow raised. Lavender resisted the urge to speak, knowing any word would pop Monica's bubble of curiosity and all her questions would spill out.

As it was, she lasted maybe a minute, her gaze darting from Lavender to Taylor's retreating form.

"Aaron told me you met a cowboy, but he didn't tell me *you* met a cowboy."

Lavender fought the blush she felt creeping up her throat. Of course it looked odd, her coming out here with Taylor.

"I told him how happy Aaron would be to get his hat back, and he offered to drive."

Monica considered her another moment. "Okay. You could have told him how to get here."

"Because it's so easy for a stranger to find this place?"

Monica swung her youngest daughter up on her hip and expertly dodged a sticky nuzzle. "It's not that hard."

"It wouldn't be if your stubborn father-in-law would let them put up street signs."

Monica tugged a wipe out of her back pocket and swiped it across her daughter's face without looking before setting the child down again. "Why are you so defensive? Honey, it's about damn time you got laid."

Lavender didn't even try to control the rush of blood this time. Even if it looked like she was interested in Taylor, who was to say he would be interested in her? Or that she'd open herself up to getting hurt like that?

Monica backed off then. "How's Gertrude?"

Great. As if she wasn't churned up enough, Monica had to mention her grandmother, who was no doubt wondering where the hell she was.

"She's good. She has her days, you know."

"I bet you'll be glad for summer, so you won't have to worry about her while you're at work."

No, she'd just have to be at her beck and call twenty-four hours a day. Lavender closed her eyes a moment and pushed back the resentment. Giving into that emotion didn't do either her or her grandmother any good.

"It will be good not to worry," Lavender admitted.

"Have you heard from your mom?"

Not in years. "Not in awhile."

"I wonder where she's landed now. I always liked her. She was so colorful, you know? She had so many neat experiences, she was always so brave, never afraid to try new things, go new places. I was always so jealous of you."

Lavender wondered how jealous she was now that Lavender was living the life of a spinster and Monica had three little kids and a husband who adored her. Sure, her mother was ready to try new things, anything that wouldn't keep her in one place too long. She hadn't been able to wait to shake the dirt of this town off her sandals, even if it meant leaving her fifteen-year-old daughter to take care of her mother after Gertrude's stroke. Every now and then her mother would come back into town just long enough to stir up that resentment again.

"Maybe we'd better go see what Aaron has got Taylor doing," Lavender suggested.

The two women strolled toward the barn. Monica never had been in a hurry to do anything. They stepped inside the barn to see Aaron holding his pony's lead in the center of the barn, Taylor crouching at the pony's flank, the animal's left hoof in the palm of his hand, his other hand pointing at Aaron. He let the hoof fall and Aaron said, "One!" Taylor picked up the hoof again, repeated the action, and Aaron crowed, "Two!"

They reached five before they noticed the women standing behind them. Taylor straightened, wiping his hands down his thighs.

"I hope that's all right, ma'am," he said to Monica. "She's a good animal, she won't hurt him."

"He's been around horses his whole life." Monica looked

past him to her son, who crouched and tried to lift the pony's foot. "It won't be the last time he's stepped on."

"Remember how I showed you," Taylor called over his shoulder. "Pinch her fetlock. Not too hard, just to show her who's boss."

Aaron apparently pinched, because the pony lifted her foot docilely.

Lavender watched Taylor with an ache in her chest. Those danged weaknesses revisited her when he met her gaze and winked. She had to get away from him, now, or nothing but pain would be in store for her.

"We should get back," she said.

He considered her a moment, then nodded slowly. "Okay." He touched his hat in Monica's direction. "Ma'am. I hope y'all come out to the rodeo this weekend and watch me ride."

Monica dimpled again. "What event are you in, Taylor?"

"Steer wrestling."

"Good luck with it. We'll try to make it out. With three kids, it's not so easy." She looked past him to Aaron. "He probably won't let us miss it, though."

"If you make it out, come say hi." He turned back to Aaron. "See you around, little man. You keep working, all right?"

Aaron was so focused on the pony, he only nodded.

"Aaron, your manners," Monica chided.

"Thank you, Mr. Craig," he said without turning around.

Taylor grinned at Lavender. "Let's head on back, then. Nice to meet you, Monica."

He rested his fingers at the small of Lavender's back, sending a shiver through her as he guided her across the yard to the truck. At the same time she wanted to lean back into his touch, wanted to see what he'd do. He held the door open and she slid in, self-conscious of his attention on her.

A few moments passed while she sought the balance she'd

had on the way out here. Surely just that little touch, that little show of possession hadn't thrown her off so far. "You were really good with him."

"I like kids. Wait, that didn't come out right." He flashed her a grin.

She smiled. "I know what you meant. But it has me wondering what you did before you decided on amateur rodeo."

His grin dimmed. "Lots of different things."

"Nothing you could settle on." Like that was a surprise. She knew his type way too well.

"Nothing that made me happy."

"And rodeo does?"

"So far."

"That's good. It's important to be happy." But like her mother, he'd probably always be chasing that happiness. She settled back in her seat and wondered why the idea made her so sad.

When he pulled up beside her Toyota, he repeated his dinner invitation.

"I can't," she said, too aware that he essentially had her trapped in the truck, and that she didn't really know him, and that the school parking lot was mostly empty, usual for the end of the school year when teachers started yearning for summer.

"Someone waiting at home?" he asked.

She wondered why he hadn't considered that before. No ring, maybe, but now she latched onto the excuse. "Yes. I'm sorry. I have to get home."

Something tightened in his face, something more than disappointment that she refused. More like disappointment in her. Her stomach twisted. She'd experienced that often enough.

He shoved open the door and climbed out. This time he didn't reach in to help her out. When she said goodbye, she didn't meet his eyes, only murmured a thank you before darting into the school to straighten her room for the next day. Regret was heavy in her heart that she'd let him believe she was taken. It had seemed the right thing to do, and going to dinner with him would only prolong her hopes, wouldn't it?

"Hey, Lavender, who was that you were talking to out there?" Jerri, one of the two third-grade teachers asked. She and the other third-grade teacher, Melissa, and the second-grade teacher, Laurie, stood in the hall by Laurie's room.

Had they been waiting for her? Lavender hated that they intimidated her. They were young and beautiful and free, everything she wasn't.

"Just a guy I met today on the field trip." She edged toward her room.

"From the rodeo?"

"Mm, yeah."

"What was he doing here?"

She waved a nonchalant hand. "Aaron left his cowboy hat behind and Mr. Craig brought it over to return it."

"Mr. Craig, hm? Well wasn't that sweet?" Laurie asked. "And you took it out to Aaron together? That's quite a distance."

"Aaron was upset about the hat, and Mr. Craig had made such an impression on him, I thought Aaron would like to thank him in person."

"Ah. So you took a forty-five-minute round trip."

Put like that, maybe it was a little foolish.

"Was the field trip fun?" Jerri asked.

Lavender rolled her eyes, grateful for the change in subject. "Are they ever?"

"If you meet guys like that, they are," Laurie sighed.

Lord, how much of Taylor had they seen?

"I need to get ready for tomorrow." Lavender opened the door to her room.

"We're going out to the Longhorn tonight," Laurie said to

her retreating back. "It's kind of a tradition during rodeo season. Do you want to come?"

Lavender turned slowly to give Jerri and Melissa enough time to give Laurie dirty looks or jabs or whatever. Lavender had stopped accepting social invitations long ago, so people had stopped inviting her. Didn't Laurie know that? In the time it took her to turn, she played all the reasons her grandmother would give for her not to go: it was a Thursday, she was too tired from her field trip, teachers going to a honky-tonk was trashy, her grandmother needed her.

But when she opened her mouth to make a more polite excuse, she pictured Taylor. She'd have a better chance of seeing him again there than by sitting home watching TV. Running into him in a dance hall wasn't the same as making plans to eat dinner with him, was it? And that little touch on the small of her back had awakened longings she'd forgotten. Yes, he would leave. Yes, it would hurt if she let it.

So instead of the, "No, thanks," she said, "What time?"

Chapter Three

Lavender hadn't been to the Longhorn in maybe ten years, but it hadn't changed much in that time. Still, she was shaking as she searched the crowd for Laurie and her friends, scanning for Taylor at the same time.

Wow, there were a lot of cowboy hats and faded jeans. Some looked good, some not so much. The bar was hidden behind rows of them, and harried waitresses rushed around with trays full of long necks. Every instinct told her to pivot and go home to her grandmother, curl up and watch TV while she recovered from the field trip.

Then she looked down the hall into the pool room and saw Taylor. He was propped against a pool cue, studying the pool table while another cowboy leaned in for a shot. He wasn't wearing his hat and his jaw-length brown hair gleamed in the dim light. He swigged a beer, then stretched out for his own shot, all delicious lean grace.

While the balls still rolled on the table, he looked up and saw her. Surprise brightened those pretty eyes, then he winked.

The ball went into the pocket and Taylor straightened with a victorious grin.

Lavender heard her name. She turned to see Laurie, Melissa and Jerri waving from a table in the middle of the main room. She edged through the crowd toward them, heart pounding. Anxiety at stepping out of her comfort zone had her nervous, not the way Taylor Craig had looked at her.

"Hey." She draped her purse over the back of the empty chair and sat, checking out the bottles on the table—three empties and three half empty. "Been here long?"

"About half an hour. We thought you wouldn't come," Jerri said.

Lavender tried not to read anything into that. "No, I wanted to. It's nice to get out."

The three women considered her a moment before Melissa leaned back to signal a waitress for another round.

"Your cowboy's here," Jerri said with a wave of her hand. "I saw him dancing earlier. He's got moves."

"He's so cute," Melissa sighed. "Too young for me, though."

Which meant too young for her by far. Lavender stiffened defensively. "He's not my cowboy." At least they couldn't see her blush in the dim light.

The band started playing a popular line dance song and the tables emptied. Her three companions popped out of their seats to join the throng on the floor. Laurie turned back to her.

"Do you know this one?"

"Um, it's been awhile. I'll watch, see if I remember."

"You're not going to remember by watching. Come on."

Laurie took her hand and pulled.

But once on the dance floor, Lavender lost her as more people crowded the floor, and she tried to follow her neighbor's feet. Strong hands closed on her hips, turning her with the crowd, and Taylor moved up beside her before releasing her.

"Watch me," he advised.

She did, studying his feet in the battered brown boots before she had to turn her back to him and follow someone else's steps, all the while self-conscious of Taylor behind her seeing her stumble, or maybe watching her big butt. Great. Her grandmother had told her the jeans were too tight.

The moves had her turning again, with Taylor to her left this time. She was finally getting it, and then the moves had him turning his back to her. She stumbled when her gaze wandered to his butt and she jerked her attention away before he turned and saw.

He grinned anyway, as if he'd known. She stuttered for a minute, then fell into step with him. The synchronicity felt good, made her feel connected to him and the dancers around. She let the music wash through her as she turned her back to him. When they were facing the same direction again, she admired his grace once more. He was light on his feet, and interpreted the rhythm more deeply than just following steps, his knees bending deeper, his hips swiveling. He even added a couple of skipping steps but kept with the beat. God, she wished she could dance like that.

The song ended just when she was starting to feel the burn in her thighs, but still she regretted leaving the floor, leaving his side. The crowd thinned as another upbeat song played and Taylor turned to her, hand outstretched, eyebrows lifted hopefully.

She backed away in horror at the fast beat. "I can't."

Regret slackened his features, and she was sorry to disappoint him. Then she saw one of the most graceful women in town at the edge of the dance floor, surrounded by men pleading for a dance, and Lavender pointed Taylor in Samantha's direction.

"She's a good dancer. Go ask her."

He looked skeptical, but apparently the music was getting to him, so he strolled over, reached through the crowd of men for Samantha and pulled her through them to swing into his arms.

Lavender burned with jealousy that she couldn't be Samantha, and then she just watched.

Samantha was as tall as Taylor, gorgeous and built, the snug clothes she wore following the line of her perfect body, her long red hair swinging behind her. Taylor curved his hand just above her waist and took her hand in his other, feet already moving in quick steps which Samantha matched for a few measures. Taylor took her in a series of quick spins in the middle of the floor before whipping her out and then back into his arms. Samantha threw back her head and laughed, and he rolled her away again, guiding her in complicated turns before pulling her back and circling with her around the floor. Their feet moved in perfect time, perfect rhythm, and Lavender marveled at how well they read each other. The floor had cleared significantly, many dancers joining her on the edge to watch. She couldn't tear her eyes away. He swung Samantha around and tucked her against his side so they circled facing the same direction before he whirled her back to face him just as the song ended.

Lavender was breathless, just watching them, and they parted, grinning. Taylor held out his hand to invite her for another dance, but Samantha shook her head.

"Samantha's rules. Only one dance," the redhead said, but Lavender thought there was regret in her friend's eyes when she turned to another partner.

Taylor turned toward Lavender then, and she realized with a jolt that he must think she was waiting for him. It was too late now to bolt back to her seat, though, so she stood, mortified, till he reached her.

"You dance so well," she managed.

"Thanks. Makes me thirsty." He tucked his hand at the small of her back and guided her to the bar.

She cast a wild-eyed glance at her colleagues, who all gave her double-thumbs up. Approval was not what she was looking for. She needed rescue.

Taylor edged sideways through the crush at the bar, anchored his elbow on the edge and looked back at her. "What'll you have?"

"I left my purse." She motioned to her table and sent another "help me" look to Laurie, who just grinned.

"I've got it." His tone was a touch impatient. "What do you want?"

When was the last time she'd even had alcohol? She had no idea what to order. She tried to remember what the other ladies were drinking but her mind was blank.

"Whatever you're having," she said finally.

He nodded his approval and ordered two Shiners. He paid and extricated himself from the crowd before handing her a bottle. "You don't want a glass or anything, do you?"

She shook her head and took a sip of the cool dark beer. No tables were available, and she didn't want to take him back to the table with the other teachers, so she leaned against a post and wondered how to escape.

"I didn't think I'd see you here," he said. "I thought you had someone waiting for you at home." His attention turned to suspicion. "It's not a cat or something, is it? And you just used it as an excuse not to have dinner with me?"

She lowered her gaze guiltily. "My grandmother. Why? Do I look like a cat lady?"

He reached over and brushed some cat hair off her fitted dark top.

"I thought I got all that," she murmured, surprised she didn't feel embarrassed that he saw her lack of perfection. "I didn't plan to come, but some of my friends invited me. And after a field trip, this is really good." She motioned with her beer and took another sip.

A corner of his mouth twitched. She really liked that twitch. "Want to dance?" he asked.

"Oh, I'm not—you saw me out there."

"Yeah, but this is the two-step. You're a Texas girl, right? You know how to two-step."

"Really, not well."

But he didn't take no for an answer. He took her beer and set it on a shelf on the post she'd been leaning on, then folded her hand in his and led her to the floor. Her heart hammered. This would not be good. She was going to make a fool of herself in front of everyone. She sucked in a breath as Taylor turned her into his arms, his hand settling lower and more centered on her than on Samantha.

Which meant their bodies were closer and she could smell him, warm and musky and male and *good*. Then they started moving and while she tried to picture herself as Samantha, she just couldn't match his steps, even though this song was nowhere near the speed of the one he'd shared with the redhead.

"Why don't you let me lead?" he bent his head to ask, a teasing note in his voice.

Embarrassment flooded her in a wave.

"Feel my hand. Let your feet follow."

Easier said than done. She stumbled after him. He slowed and simplified his steps, but the damage was done. She was mortified, but he wouldn't let her escape. His patience only made it worse.

She'd never been so glad for a song to end. She broke away, not meeting his eyes.

"Thanks for the beer."

"Where you going?"

"I'm more tired than I thought. I... Thank you." She turned and wove through tables to where Melissa sat alone. Laurie and Jerri were dancing. She unlooped her purse from the back of her chair, made her excuses and bolted from the Longhorn Saloon.

Chapter Four

AH, yes, another exciting Friday afternoon grocery shopping at the Handy Andy with her grandmother. Gertrude Cates insisted on the weekly outing to beat the Saturday crowds. Lavender hadn't really minded until today. She wanted to be anywhere but in public.

Jerri, Melissa and Laurie had been waiting for her when she got to school this morning and she'd cursed herself for not giving into the desire to take a personal day. But that would have been the coward's way out and she'd used up her allotment of coward last night.

"Where'd you run off to last night?" Jerri had asked.

"You looked completely freaked out," Melissa added. "What did he do to you?"

Nothing. She hadn't given him time to do anything. She'd berated herself all night, consoling herself that she'd never see him again.

Lavender had turned away and unlocked her classroom door. "I hadn't realized how tired I was."

"You didn't look tired. You looked upset. Like he'd upset you."

"I just felt ridiculous," Lavender admitted, though saying it aloud made her sick. She didn't know these women well enough to know if they'd hold her confession against her, but clearly they weren't going to leave her alone till she said something. "He's so young and he bought me a beer and was flirting with me. I felt like he was making fun of me."

"Why would he do that?" Laurie asked, her tone shrill with concern.

"It was just a feeling."

Melissa shook her head. "He asked me to dance and didn't buy me a beer. He asked me about you."

Lavender reddened. God only knew what Melissa told him, and she didn't want to ask. She didn't want to read anything into his curiosity. She was never going to see him again, remember? And if she wondered what he saw in her, didn't they? She'd never been so glad to hear the bell signaling the start of classes.

She lost her grandmother in the store, which was a trick since it was only ten aisles. She was pretty sure she'd left her back in the jelly aisle trying to decide if she wanted to buy a new flavor or stick with the same strawberry preserves she always bought. She'd get the preserves. Gertrude Cates was the one member of her family who acted with any kind of predictability.

Lavender turned her cart back around, her list done, and her heart jolted when she saw a lean cowboy surrounded by several older women, including her grandmother.

Gertrude's voice carried down the aisle as she gestured to Taylor's hand basket. "What kind of meal do you think you're eating there? That's nothing for a growing boy to eat—no nutrition at all."

Despite her better judgment, Lavender crept closer to see what products had earned Gertrude's ire. Macaroni and cheese, beanie weenies—she didn't even know they made those anymore —Pop Tarts. She was right. He was a child.

"Now, ma'am, I'm fully grown." Taylor's deep voice carried, too, and hit a chord in Lavender that had her vibrating with an energy she didn't want to name.

"You'll hardly stay healthy enough eating like that. What you need is a good home cooked meal," one of Gertrude's friends, Corrinna, chided.

"It's been awhile since I've had one of those," he admitted.

"Gertrude is a very good cook," another friend, Fiona, chimed in. "And she's training her granddaughter to do the same. You can't find many young women who like to cook these days."

Old busybody. Where was she going with this?

"Granddaughter, hm?" And as if he'd known she'd been standing behind him the whole time, Taylor turned and smiled, not even bothering to look surprised. "Hey, where'd you run off to last night?"

Past him, Gertrude stiffened.

"I was more tired than I thought after that field trip." Lavender approached cautiously, not sure who to be more wary of. Maybe he'd buy her excuse even though the other teachers hadn't.

His gaze traveled lazily over her. "All rested now?"

She lifted her chin and pushed her hair back, aware of the trio of elderly ladies watching. "Yes, teaching a roomful of five-year- olds is better than yoga."

He laughed. "I hear you're a good cook."

She used every ounce of concentration not to blush. "I am a very good cook."

"As you can see," he lifted his basket for her inspection. "I am not. These ladies seem to believe you'll cook for me."

When she looked into those grey eyes, she couldn't form the

word "no." Where had that word disappeared to? Instead, she said, "Do you like lasagna?"

"You know that boy?" Gertrude demanded once they'd brought the groceries into the house. She was too much of a lady to contradict Lavender's invitation once issued, but she was upset.

"I met him at the rodeo yesterday. He showed us his horse."

"And he's the reason you wanted to go out last night even though you never go out with your friends."

She didn't even have friends, really, but didn't say so. "Yes, ma'am." No point in lying now.

"And you told him to finagle an invitation to dinner?"

"No, ma'am!" Lavender set the canned tomatoes on the counter with a thunk. "I don't know how he knew that we'd be there."

"But you think he was there for you?"

Lavender turned to put the butter in the refrigerator. "That would be arrogant of me, wouldn't it?"

"Lavender, you know what kind of people those rodeo riders are. People who can't settle down, who shake the dust off their feet when they leave a town."

"Like my parents." Her tone was sharper than she intended, and pain creased her grandmother's face.

"You've been hurt enough by that type. Why would you think about getting involved with these people?"

Because she'd stopped being a victim a long time ago, and had learned to appreciate her life, filling all the holes. "I'm not involved with anyone. I danced with him. Once. And not well."

"I saw the way he looked at you, Lavender."

"I'm not responsible for that. And you're the one inviting strange men to dinner, so either help or get out of the kitchen."

Gertrude eyed the lasagna ingredients on the counter, then propped her hands on her hips. "You're better at the Italian than me." So she got out of the kitchen.

There hadn't been a man in the house since...well, unless you counted the plumber, who was in his fifties and putting two kids through college, or the air conditioning guy, who was younger than her, happily married to his high school sweetheart and had four kids...since she couldn't remember. Or wouldn't remember. Even if there were available men in Cascade, other than the transient cowboys, she didn't have a place for them.

Lavender was studying the cabinet, trying to decide what to make for dessert and thinking about how nice it was to cook for someone else for a change when a quiet knock came at the kitchen door. She leaned back to look around the open cabinet door and saw Taylor standing on the other side of the screen, a pink bakery box in one hand, a bottle of wine in the other.

"I hope you haven't made dessert," he said, brushing past her as she held the screen door open for him.

He smelled delicious, the scent she'd noticed last night layered beneath Ivory soap, shaving cream—was there a more delicious smell?—and shampoo. And that was beyond the rich scent of chocolate coming from the box.

"I was just trying to figure out what to make. You didn't have to bring anything."

"Good manners, right? When I passed by the bakery, I saw this cake." He set it down on the counter and motioned for her to open it.

She untapped it gingerly and peeled back the top to reveal a fudge coated layer cake.

"Mm. Big sweet tooth?" She smiled.

"Oh, yeah."

"Well, I hope you have enough room after my lasagna." She nodded toward the noodles boiling on the stove, the sauce cooking beside it.

"What can I do to help?"

"You don't have to."

"Lavender." He tucked a strand of hair behind her ear. "Just because I'm a guy doesn't mean I'm helpless in the kitchen. What can I do to help?"

She slipped out of his reach, watched the strands of hair fall from his fingertips, then sucked in a deep breath to focus. "Can you grate cheese?"

He eased back, relaxed in victory. "I can do that."

She gathered the supplies he'd need, grateful. She hated to grate cheese, always worried about scraping her fingers on the grater.

Taylor, however, used it with confident, long strokes. His hands mesmerized her.

"Why don't you use a food processor?" he asked.

"I hate cleaning it."

She stirred the sauce, then got salad ingredients from the fridge, and checked the noodles. Good, they were ready. Removing them with her tongs, she began layering them into the pan.

"So did you know who Gertrude was when you started talking to her?"

"Who's Gertrude?" He placed the bowl of cheese on the counter beside her and hefted the head of Romaine. "What do you want me to do with this?"

"Rinse it, then you can start tearing it into the bowl on the top of the refrigerator there. Gertrude is my grandmother. Did you know that when you started talking to her?"

"No, I didn't know who she was. And she and her friends started talking to me."

"Ah."

"I did know you would be there, though."

She whipped around to look at him. "Are you kidding?"

"No. Everyone knows you shop after school on Friday. I wanted to find you and apologize for whatever I did to upset you last night."

She rested a hip against the counter and waved her tongs at him. "So you weren't really buying that stuff? You were just trying to find me?"

"Oh, sure, I bought the stuff. I cook sometimes in the RV." He rinsed off the lettuce and started tearing.

She turned back to the lasagna, aware her next question would open her up to more questions than she might want to share the answer to. "So why did you think you upset me?"

"You left in kind of a hurry, and you didn't look too happy. I thought I'd done something wrong, and I want to apologize."

She shook her head. "It's not you. I'm just not very good out of my element."

"So why did you go last night?"

"I was invited. Not a usual occasion."

"Why not?"

"I say no too much. People stop asking."

"Why do you say no?"

"I have other responsibilities." Not that he would understand that.

"What, your grandmother?" He glanced toward the door where she'd disappeared. "She seems fine to me."

"She has her days. And when her schedule is disrupted she gets agitated. When I got home last night she was a mess." Why was she telling him this? "Sorry. Not your problem."

"I asked," he replied easily. "Alzheimer's?"

She shook her head. "She had a stroke when I was in high

school. She never fully recovered and can't really be on her own."

"So where's the rest of your family?"

"God knows."

He stopped tearing and looked at her. "Are you kidding?"

"Nope. No idea where they are." She finished layering the lasagna and slid it into the oven. "Are you okay with that?" She gestured to the lettuce.

"Sure, I got it."

She reached for another bowl and pulled out ingredients for the salad dressing. "She can't eat raw eggs, so I have another recipe for Caesar salad."

"What does she do while you're at school?"

"She stays here. The neighbors keep an eye out."

"And last night?"

"She stayed here. She wasn't happy about it."

"Where is she now?"

"Taking a nap in front of Jeopardy, probably."

Taylor finished the lettuce, wiped his hands on a towel. "So without you—?"

"She'd be in a home. Don't make me a hero," she said quickly, seeing the contemplative look he slid her way.

He nodded and stepped back. "You got a corkscrew, or do you want to wait for dinner?"

"The drawer to your right there." Maybe a glass of wine would settle her nerves, though honestly she wasn't as nervous as she'd thought. He was easy to talk to. And she had hardly thought about those long hands and how they'd felt when he danced with her last night.

"Wine glasses?"

"Right above you there." She pointed to the cabinet by the refrigerator.

"You think your grandmother wants some?"

"Maybe just a little glass with dinner. So, what's your story? You have mine. What do you do when you're not steer wrestling?" She grinned just saying the words. "I don't think I've ever asked anyone that before."

He handed her a glass of wine and leaned back against the counter with his own glass. "I work a ranch near Alpine."

"Alpine. Can you believe I've lived in Texas all my life and I've never been there? Is it pretty?"

"Prettiest land you ever saw." He smiled. "You should come up."

"Right." Just what she wanted to go visit some cowboy in a bunkhouse someplace she'd never been. Despite herself she could imagine snuggling up in a narrow bed with him, looking out over the wild land.

Who was she kidding? She had no idea what a bunkhouse was like, and she had no business imagining herself in his bed, in his arms. No business imaging leaving this place.

"Tell me about it."

"It's great." A smile wreathed his face as his eyes took a faraway look as he described it, the open desert, the mountains, hot days, chilly nights. Again she thought about being wrapped in his arms as they looked out over the scenery.

"It's the most beautiful place I've ever been," he said, his low voice taking on a dreamy quality.

"Have you been a lot of places?"

The pleasure in his eyes dimmed. "A few."

"I imagine, with the rodeo."

Now the line of his mouth thinned. "Yeah."

"So why do you leave so often if you love it so much?"

"I love this, too. A competitive streak, I guess."

"Really." She lifted her eyebrows.

"Mostly against myself, though."

"Sure." She moved toward the sink to start rinsing the sauce pot. "So if I was to challenge you to a game of poker, say..."

He sidled over and nudged her aside with a bump of his hip and took the pot from her, grinning. "Oh, I'd try to win."

LAVENDER BENT over to get the lasagna out of the oven. Taylor leaned back to enjoy the view of that curvy bottom in those snug dark jeans, and received a smart rap with a spoon on his knuckles. Gertrude, seated to his left at the table, scowled when he snatched his hand away.

"We did not invite you here for that."

"Yes, ma'am," he said politely. "It's just a nice benefit."

Lavender carried the casserole to the table and looked from one to the other. "What?"

Taylor folded his hands on the table and smiled. "Nothing."

She glanced at her grandmother. "Uh-huh. You need anything else while I'm up?"

"Just for you to sit down." He reached for the serving spoon and held out a hand for Gertrude's plate.

"We pray first in our home, Mr. Craig," Gertrude said.

Well, she wasn't the friendly old lady she'd been in the store anymore, was she? All because she caught him staring at Lavender's behind.

Well, she probably knew what he'd been thinking, too.

He set the spoon down and the women each reached a hand toward him. He took each and bowed his head, not thinking about the words Gertrude spoke, but of the soft hand in his right, and even when Gertrude was done and he'd raised his head, he was reluctant to release Lavender.

She realized it and blushed, tugging free. Taylor picked up

the spoon again, took Gertrude's plate before she could protest, and dug out the exact piece she wanted.

When he turned to get Lavender's plate he saw a look in her eyes that sent a jolt through him, a tenderness, a longing that he understood too well. How much did they have in common?

~

AFTER DINNER, Gertrude stood up. "I'm going to take my bath and watch my show. You need to go now," she told Taylor.

"Grandma," Lavender chided. "Taylor brought us a beautiful chocolate cake from Daisy's. Don't you want a slice with a glass of milk?"

"Good Lord, no. Do you know how much butter that girl puts in her cakes? It would clog my arteries while I'm sleeping."

"More for us, then." Lavender stood, too, and gathered the dishes.

Taylor jumped to his feet to take them from her. She hesitated, then let him. Gertrude made a disapproving sound, and shuffled out of the room.

"You want milk with your cake, Taylor?"

He reached for the bottle of wine, divided the last of it between them. "Why don't we let the lasagna settle, go sit outside or something?"

She glanced at the dishes in the sink.

"They'll keep."

After a moment, she nodded and picked up her wine glass.

"We have a screened porch in the back."

"Lead the way."

She did, out the back door and down a couple of steps to a saltillo tiled patio. Two big Adirondack chairs were positioned to look out through screens onto a triangular lawn lined with blooming rose bushes.

Taylor walked to the back door and stared. "Who does that?"

"Does what?" Lavender stopped herself from sitting in one of the chairs and joined him.

"Takes care of the flowers."

"Oh, me."

"Can we go out there?"

"Sure, the mosquitoes will stop chewing on us after the blood is gone."

He huffed a laugh through his nose but pushed the door open. "They won't like us after all the garlic in the sauce anyway."

"You know, I've never found that to be true." But she followed him anyway.

The St. Augustine grass was thick beneath his boots and the scent of roses carried on the gentle breeze. He'd never really liked the smell, but the riot of colors combined with it made him smile now. Lavender wandered over and snapped off a fading flower, brought the petals to her nose, then let them scatter.

"You do all this," he said.

She shrugged. "It's therapy. Keeps me busy."

He could hear the loneliness in her voice and it hit him, low. He didn't want to ask if there'd been someone special in her life, didn't want to think about someone walking away from her because of her responsibilities.

He took her hand, lifted her palm to his face and inhaled. She curled her fingers inward to resist his touch. Tension ran from her wrist up her arm but she didn't pull away. The set of her jaw and the shadow in her eyes told him she wanted to, and that she didn't want to.

Her wariness didn't deter and he gave a little tug, so she didn't misunderstand his intention.

"Taylor," she murmured, all pink again.

"Why not?"

She gave a little shiver that only firmed his determination to taste her, to touch her.

"You make me want things I can't have."

She was close enough now that her breath brushed his lips, sending a surge of lust south.

"You can tonight," he murmured, and with only a slight shift, brought his mouth to hers.

A soft little moan vibrated against his mouth as he parted her lips with his, felt the rush of her wine-scented breath. He threaded his fingers through her hair, finding it as silky as he imagined, her cheek beneath as soft.

So long, so long since she'd been touched, held, kissed, and God, if she was going to break a drought, Taylor Craig was the man to do it with. The man could kiss, his firm lips fitting over hers, moving with hers, his tongue making gentle explorations as he curved his hand around the back of her neck and stroked her cheek with his thumb.

She could stand for hours, breathing him, tasting him, and he seemed just as content, even when he angled his head to deepen the kiss, bring her a step closer.

Just when she decided to slide her hand up his chest–firm, muscular, his heart thumping steadily beneath her palm–itching to touch his hair, slide it between her fingers, she realized she still held her wine glass.

She didn't want to. Every nerve in her screamed not to, that this wouldn't happen again. Still, she drew back from the kiss. Not too far back, because of the way he was looking at her, those light eyes all focused and wanting and questioning. She reached for his glass. He took her glass from her, tossed the wine out onto the roses and dropped the glasses onto the thick carpet grass before slipping one hand around the small of her back and the other into her hair and pulling her all against the hard length of him, kissing her till she was dizzier than the wine could ever make her. She wound her arms around his neck and held on, toying with the ends of his hair, pressing her palms to the warm skin of his neck.

Then he slid that hand up her side, along her breast, and swept his thumb over her nipple.

It was like flipping a switch. Everything she'd sublimated for the past few years poured forth, a hunger she'd forgotten, unquenchable, uncontrollable. She pressed closer to him, to his hand, her own tongue demanding in his mouth, now, both hands linked around his neck to hold her to him. They were so close and she could feel the ridge of his desire. She moved against it till he moaned into her mouth, released her breast to settle both hands on her hips.

"Inside," he whispered, his tone choked.

And that was a dash of cold water. She stepped back, her whole body tingling. "I can't. Not here."

His eyes had gone smoky with desire, no longer focused. Well, probably focused on something in the future, not on reasoning out what she was saying. "Why not?"

"My grandmother."

His eyes focused a little more. "Where, then?"

His hands rested on her hips but she could imagine them wandering her body, lingering. Where could they go?

Just when she was about to throw good sense to the wind and drag him down to the grass just to feel him over her, her grandmother opened the back door.

"Are you two going to eat this cake or not?"

Chapter Five

Lavender flipped through a magazine as she sat in the waiting area of Wild Hair, Cascade's salon, and tried not to think of Taylor. She could still taste him, still feel his hands, the length of his body.

Every part of her was awake now, every dormant hormone wanted to come out and play.

With Taylor.

He'd given her wicked looks when they joined Gertrude in the kitchen, and Lavender had waited for Gertrude to say something because even if Taylor didn't look like he'd been thoroughly kissed, she knew she did. But Gertrude hadn't even acted suspicious, though Taylor had kept teasing with his laughing eyes and long looks and lingering touches.

She'd been one giant nerve by the time she'd walked him out to his truck. The sun had gone down, which meant the evening had cooled enough for her neighbors to be out in full force for their evening walks. Several of them called out and waved, slowing for a better look at the man coming out of her house.

Taylor must have sensed her tension because he didn't

throw her down on the hood of the truck and have his way with her.

Instead, he climbed in and leaned on the open window to look at her.

"Come watch me ride tomorrow."

She hadn't even tried to come up with an excuse. Instead, flushed with pleasure, she'd said, "okay."

He'd glanced about at the curious walkers, winked and driven off.

And she'd run into the house to make this appointment. She hadn't factored in how busy the place would be the day before Mother's Day.

"So who was that cowboy?" Mrs. Patterson asked, settling into a chair beside her.

Lavender jolted. Had Mrs. Patterson been one of the walkers out last night? "What cowboy?" Dummy. Everyone would know she was buying time, and at least a dozen people had seen Taylor leaving her house last night.

"The one feeling you up in your roses last night." Mrs. Patterson said it so loud everyone in the shop turned to stare. Mrs. Patterson beamed, pleased with the attention her scoop had garnered.

Lavender's ears buzzed as blood rushed in them. It was the only sound in the shop for a moment, then the place exploded in conversation.

"Lavender? A cowboy?"

"From the Longhorn? I heard you were dancing with someone there."

"Lavender doesn't go to the Longhorn."

"Who is he? He was a cutie. A little young, though."

How did she even start to answer? She didn't know what was going on with Taylor, and what she did know she didn't want to share. She knew it was foolish, but once again, she took the coward's way out and bolted.

And collided with Samantha Starr right on the sidewalk. The redhead cocked a hip and looked from Lavender to the door.

"They didn't try to talk you into a perm, did they?"

Lavender scooped her hair back but didn't meet Samantha's eyes. "Too many people." Wanting to know too much about her.

Samantha turned an assessing gaze to Lavender's straight hair. "And you want to fancy yourself up for the cowboy."

Lavender stiffened and prepared to walk off, but Samantha reached out and threaded a lock of hair through two fingers.

"I can fix you up."

Lavender hesitated, vanity battling with a need to hide away. "Really?"

"Sure. I did in for the other girls when I was in Vegas all the time. I thought maybe I'd add a chair or two to my spa, you know, just for an alternative. What about it?"

Lavender looked over her shoulder at the crowded salon, then back at Samantha, who always looked amazing. "Okay."

SAMANTHA SAT Lavender in a chair in the back of the building she was renovating and dragged her basket of supplies close. She flipped the protective sheet around Lavender and fastened it around her neck.

"I just want you to give it some shape." Lavender fingered her hair and dragged it forward. "It won't do much anyway, it's so straight and fine."

Samantha threaded the hair through her fingers, considering, before pinning up strands with the plastic clips. Lavender's heart skipped. "Not too short, okay?"

"Trust me." Samantha combed out the loose hair, picked up the scissors and got to work. "Are you going to the rodeo today?"

"I think I might."

Samantha's lips quirked as she flicked a glance to Lavender in the mirror. "When was the last time you went?"

"Not counting with my class? About ten years ago."

"I wonder why you decided to go now." Samantha's eyes glinted.

"He...asked me."

"Really." Samantha's voice rose in interest. "How long has it been?"

Lavender didn't pretend not to know what Samantha meant. She hadn't thought of much else since that kiss last night. She knew how long it had been to the minute, but all she said was, "A long long time."

"And this is the guy you danced with night before last?"

"If you could call it dancing. You danced with him, too."

"Yep. The boy can move. And he sure is pretty, those light eyes and dark eyelashes. Nice haircut, too. Not cheap."

Interesting. To Lavender, it had just looked like he was letting his hair grow out, that he didn't have the time or money to go get it trimmed.

She sighed and started to relax for the first time since she'd decided to go to the rodeo. She didn't have many friends she trusted enough to talk to, but Samantha had some life experience. Lavender envied her that. "I wish I could dance like you. He said I was leading."

"It's not hard. Guys just mostly want to get their hands on you anyway they can. They don't care how you dance."

Lavender stopped herself from shaking her head in disagreement. That would be a good way to ruin her haircut. "You said yourself he has moves. I want to be able to move with him." An idea almost made her bounce in her chair—another bad idea. "Can you show me?"

"Lavender, I've been dancing for a long time."

"I know. I know I can't move like you, but I want to be able to move with him. Can you show me?"

Samantha met her eyes in the mirror again and bit her lip. Lavender knew she was asking a lot of the woman who already had too many irons in the fire, starting her own business, but Lavender was desperate. She didn't have long – he'd be leaving tomorrow with the rest of the cowboys. And she wanted to feel graceful in his arms just once.

If she could only think of how she could leave Gertrude for another evening.

"All right, fine, come back after the rodeo. I'll give you about an hour. Wear whatever shoes you'll be dancing in."

Lavender was shaking with giddiness as she left the shop. She knew just who to ask to stay with Gertrude tonight.

Her neighbor across the street, Mrs. Aguilar smiled when she opened the door. She was the one Lavender depended on most to help her with Gertrude during the school year.

Lavender looked down at the tiny woman, a contemporary of her mother's, a woman who had stayed behind in Cascade when her children left. "Mrs. Aguilar, I have a huge favor to ask." But she asked anyway.

Mrs. Aguilar patted her arm. "It's no problem. We'll play cards. Gertrude likes that. Sweetie, you've given up so much. You should go out and have fun."

"I can't – I don't know – it'll be late." Please, God.

"Once she's in bed, I can go home. You don't worry. You go, you have fun."

Lavender hugged her in thanks and nearly danced all the way home.

Maybe she had some rhythm after all.

THE RODEO WAS PACKED and loud and dusty. The scent of grease from the concessions washed the air and Lavender gained ten pounds just thinking about a corn dog and a funnel cake. Instead, she bought a beer in a big plastic cup and made her way to the stands, scanning the dirt arena for a glimpse of Taylor. Would he be out here, or was there a backstage kind of thing somewhere? Would she know him by the way he moved? Probably. Her heart thudded at the idea of seeing him, at him seeing her.

One of the high school teachers waved, and Lavender considered going to sit with her, but she wanted to focus on Taylor when he came out. She didn't want small talk distracting her. So she waved back and gave her attention to the arena.

The color guard rode out on horses with the American flag and the Texas flag, and Deb Lawson, the high school music teacher, stepped to the center of the arena to sing the national anthem. Annie's husband Chad looked on with their two-month old daughter in his arms, and Lavender choked up at the sweetness of his expression.

She found her seat again for the bareback competition. Her neck hurt just watching the way the cowboys flopped on the backs of the horses.

Then, on the outside of the arena, across from the stands, she saw Angelina's gleaming mane. Her heart gave a big thump as she searched for Taylor, saw him, head bent under a straw cowboy hat as he listened to another cowboy who talked with his hands. Taylor nodded, then nodded again, his hand resting on the pommel of Angelina's saddle. He lifted his head and Lavender wished she'd thought to bring binoculars. How ridiculous in an arena where she was so close, but she didn't want to miss his expressions, didn't want to miss anything.

And yes, she was being ridiculous.

A cheer went up as the next bareback rider made it to eight seconds, and the event was over.

"Next up, steer wrestling," the announcer drawled.

Across the arena, Taylor swung into the saddle. Lavender's mouth went dry and she took a quick sip of beer.

But he wasn't first. A man twice Taylor's size, who dwarfed his poor horse, was the first out of the chute, and dropped over the steer with a death grip on the short horns. Using his weight and strength, he nearly twisted the poor animal's head off before dropping him to the dirt.

4.4 seconds from the start of the ride to the steer's feet leaving the ground. Wow, that was fast. And he was big. The announcer kept saying so. How much of an advantage was that over Taylor?

Taylor wasn't next, either. Another big guy, but the steer got away from him. He never even got out of the saddle.

Taylor still wasn't next. Lavender shifted on the hard seat. This next guy was faster than the first, dropping out of his saddle and onto the steer in 3.8 seconds.

And then Angelina stepped into the chute.

"Next up is newcomer to the sport, Taylor Craig," drawled the announcer. "He's not a very big fella. These steer outweigh him three to one. He hasn't finished in the money yet this year. Maybe this week is his chance."

Taylor pressed his hat more firmly onto his head, took a firmer grip on Angelina's reins, tensed his shoulders, and the chute sprung open. Lavender only got to admire him astride the galloping mare for a moment before he slid off the other side. Angelina kept going and Taylor dug his heels into the dirt, legs spread as he leaned into the steer, the muscles in his arms standing out as he twisted and the animal fell beneath him.

He got up with a satisfied nod when he heard his time of 4.2

seconds and went to retrieve his hat, which had flown off the moment Angelina left the chute. He dusted it against his leg, put it back on and lifted his head to look straight at her. He gave her a slow smile, touched his hat and strode out of the arena.

Lavender watched the other contestants in the event with a sense of pride in Taylor, as nearly all fell short of his time, and he came in third place. She sought him along the opposite side of the corral, wanting to watch him as the standings were announced, but she didn't see him. Still, she whooped, knowing she drew attention but not caring.

Well, not much.

Out of the corner of her eye, she saw the high school teacher approaching. She grumbled under her breath, not wanting to make conversation.

"Hey."

Taylor swung up on the seat beside her, eyes alight, holding his hat in one hand between his parted knees. Sweat dampened his hair and shirt, and he smelled like horse and hay and Taylor.

"Hey." Giddiness bubbled up in her. "Congratulations."

"Thanks," He glanced around. "Got a kiss for the third place winner?"

She dipped her head for a minute. Why did she have to be such a wimp around him? So she lifted her face, scooped her fingers through his hair and kissed him softly, her lips parted over his, enough to draw in his surprised breath. She broke the kiss and smiled into his eyes.

"Congratulations." She dropped her hand away from where she played with the ends of his hair.

Just when she would pull back, he threaded his fingers through her hair. "I've been wanting to smell you all day. Looks nice, by the way."

"Thanks." She blushed. "What do you mean you've been wanting to smell me?"

He bent his head close to her shoulder and breathed in deep. "You smell good. Roses, something else, I don't know. Like you."

She realized then that they were nearly nuzzling each other in public. Their knees touched, their heads were bent together.

"You want to come say hi to Angelina?"

She glanced at the arena where the team ropers were competing. Her nerves buzzed.

"Yeah. I would."

He folded his hand around hers and she followed him down the steps, under the seats and toward the stables. Angelina was in her stall. Taylor opened it quickly, one handed, and pulled Lavender inside.

Angelina tossed her head and backed away when Taylor turned Lavender and pinned her against the inside of the stall, braced his arms on either side of her and lowered his mouth to hers, warm and slick. The hunger rose fast, from anticipation to lust in a microsecond and she angled her head to bring him deeper. He made a sound of approval and eased closer, his hips pressed to hers, easing her thighs apart.

His scent surrounded her, his taste filled her, his body, so lean and strong, pinned her. Again and again she saw the flex of his muscles as he threw that steer to the ground. She wound her arms around his neck to comb through his hair and still he didn't touch her. She thought about sliding her hands down his arms and bringing his hands to her body, but realized he was savoring her, taking his time, as if they had some.

So she would do the same, enjoy every minute, every touch, every sensation he awakened in her.

No telling how much time had passed before he eased away, his breathing heavy, eyes a little glassy. She wanted to drag him back but stopped.

"You want to get something to eat?" he asked.

And ruin the perfectly good taste of Taylor in her mouth? Not likely. Ooh, a Taylor diet. Now that held appeal. With a shock, she remembered she was supposed to meet Samantha for a dance lesson. What had she been thinking, an hour away from Taylor? Of course, she hadn't known they'd be making out in his horse's stall.

"I can't. I have to be somewhere."

Disappointment dimmed his grin. "Gertrude?"

"Actually, no. Something else." With every ounce of will she had, she eased toward the stall door, wondering just how debauched she looked. "Will you be at the Longhorn later?"

Surprise lifted his eyebrows. "Will you? I got the impression you didn't really like it there."

"I'll make an exception for you." She unhooked the latch on the door. "And I'll even let you lead."

Chapter Six

Taylor saw her the minute she walked into the Longhorn Saloon, and he hadn't been watching. He'd been playing pool with his hazer, Alex Adams, and he swore he smelled Lavender. She looked different than she had the first night he'd seen her. Apart from the fitted top that showed off her gorgeous curves, ones he'd used every bit of control not to caress earlier today, he couldn't say what was different. The stylish haircut, all that pretty blonde hair in layers, wasn't the difference, or the dramatic way she'd made up her eyes. Tonight there was a glow, a playfulness about her, which he'd seen in her that first day with her class. The thing that had drawn him to her in the first place.

"Taylor, your shot," Alex said.

Taylor grunted and handed over his cue, his focus on the woman by the door.

She turned just then, and that smile... Well, it would be a shame to wipe that smile from that mouth, but he needed to claim her, needed to taste her. Had it only been a couple of hours since he'd seen her?

Surprise flickered in her eyes in the instant before he curved his hand around the small of her back and leaned in for a kiss, resisting the urge to linger. Her eyes were bright, her cheeks pink, when he drew back and without a word, guided her out of the poolroom and up to the bar.

Other men were looking at her, studying her, some with looks on their faces as if they'd never seen her before. Taylor edged closer, his thigh touching hers as he leaned sideways to order two bottles of beer. He turned back to her and guided her to a tall table, helped her perch on a stool. He didn't take his hand from her, stroked her arm below the sleeve of her blouse. They hadn't spoken since she came in, hadn't needed to. The way she smiled at him, the promise there, gave him a buzz stronger than any beer.

A song he loved played, a song that made him want to move his feet and he straightened in invitation. Anxiety flashed across Lavender's face as she glanced at the dance floor, and he remembered how resistant she'd been in his arms when they'd danced. She wasn't accustomed to a song like this.

"Dance with Samantha again," she said, nodding toward the stunning redhead he'd danced with the other night.

He took both her hands in his. "I want to dance with you."

She looked toward the floor. "I've been practicing but I'm not that good. Go dance with her. I like to watch you move."

"What every man likes to hear." He grabbed the seat of her stool and dragged her closer, between his parted legs. "But the only woman I want in my arms tonight is you." He lowered his chin to her shoulder and looked up into her face.

She twisted her head to meet his gaze. "You want to dance."

"Love this song."

She took a deep breath. "Okay."

"Yeah?" He was on his feet before she could change her mind.

He didn't even wait for her to take his hand, just grabbed

hers. "I'm not even close to good," she protested as he backed her toward the floor.

"Just relax and follow me." He lifted his arm and twisted her wrist just a bit so that she turned under his arm. He pulled her back, flush against his body. "See? Better already." He spread his hand over the small of her back, wanting the softness of her body against his. "Have fun."

Her first few steps were off, her body tight with anxiety, but he pressed his fingers into her waist and she fell into step. Her eyes brightened as they moved around the floor in rhythm. One song blended into the other and Lavender tossed her head back and laughed.

He pulled her close. "I'm going to spin you now."

Anxiety widened her eyes. "I'm not ready for that."

"Trust me. Have fun." And with a flex of his fingers, he pushed her away, twisting her hand in his to spin her in a circle. She stumbled a bit, but laughed and flung her hand out in a flourish before he pulled her back against him. Again she stumbled. This time, he took her in tight little circles, making her laugh more, but she kept up. He grinned at the victory he saw in her eyes.

At the next line dance, he guided her back to their table, where their beer had grown warm. He flagged down a waitress and ordered two more. Lavender's face was flushed but her eyes were alight with happiness. The sight sent an unfamiliar warmth through him.

"Fun, right?" he asked.

"I may be addicted."

"Lavender, hey!"

The women she'd been with the first night here approached and arranged themselves in various poses as they stood beside Lavender. He looked from them to Lavender, whose radiant expression had dimmed. Taylor gave her a teasing smile and she relaxed a bit.

"Jerri, Susan and Laurie, this is Taylor."

"Hi, Taylor," they said together.

"Y'all look good out there," said the blonde who appeared to be their spokesperson. Taylor wondered a moment, given his affinity for blondes, if he'd seen her first, would he have asked her to come see him ride?

He hadn't asked a woman to come watch him ride, not in months. But he'd asked Lavender. He wanted to be with Lavender. He reached across and to rub the tips of his fingers over the back of her hand and her eyes lit up again.

"We were good out there." He eased back to pay the waitress and handed Lavender her bottle, letting his touch linger on her fingers. The smile she gave him was brilliant and held just a bit of laughter, as if she understood his claim.

Reluctantly he dragged his attention to her friends, aware he was being rude, not much caring. "Ladies," he said. "Did you make it to the rodeo today?"

"Not really our thing." Jerri leaned on the table between them, arms folded under her breasts, pushing them up.

He took a swig of beer. "Lavender didn't think it was her thing either, but she had fun."

"From what I saw." She grinned at him, then turned to her friends. "It was fun, though. Taylor got third place."

"What is it you do, Taylor?" Susan asked.

"I'm a steer wrestler."

All four women looked at his arms.

A new song started, slow and easy and all Taylor could think about was feeling Lavender's body up against him. He straightened. "Sorry, ladies, this is our song." He reached across for Lavender's hand, lifted it over Laurie's head and guided her to the floor.

"We don't have a song," Lavender murmured when he pulled her close.

"Just wanted to hold you against me."

She folded her arms around his shoulders, pressing her soft curves against his chest. "You've been holding me against you all night."

"Mm, not like this." Her body was tense, as if she expected to start two-stepping, but he linked his hands around her waist, over the small of her back. "Just sway with me."

"This isn't dancing. It's foreplay."

He grinned and moved his hands over her back. "Yep."

She drew in a breath as he brushed his cheek along hers, his breath stirring her hair. He kissed her jaw lightly and she went tense, hopefully for a whole other reason. He kissed below her ear and she stopped moving. He chuckled against her skin and pressed his hands to her back to get her going again. When he raised his head to look at her, her eyes were dark with anticipation, her lips parted, and he couldn't resist. He kissed her softly, dipping his tongue between those full lips briefly before lifting his head again.

"Have we got part two of this plan worked out?" she asked breathlessly.

"No rooms at the motel."

Her mouth curved down in disappointment.

"I have an RV, but it has a rotten bed, not long enough, not very comfortable. I want you in a real bed."

Her eyes flashed at that, but he couldn't identify the emotion. Then she lowered her eyes. "It doesn't matter. I can't stay the night anyway. I actually didn't think we'd be here this long."

He grinned. "You thought I'd just sweep you out the door the minute you walked in?"

"The way you were kissing me earlier? Yeah."

"Do you want to go?"

This time he could read the emotion in her eyes—nervousness.

She tightened her arms about him a bit. "I'm having fun."

"Good." But he wanted that out-of-focus look in her eyes again, so he brought her closer and kissed her, deeper this time, longer, until the song changed. "You let me know when you're ready to go."

Lavender swallowed hard, the kiss still buzzing through her blood cells. If they left now, which her whole body was chanting for her to do, everyone would know why. Heck, everyone had probably figured it out anyway, after that kiss. And she didn't want to run out of time, didn't want to feel rushed when they were alone.

"You want to go with this one?" he asked, inclining his head toward the band, now playing a more up-tempo song, and they still swayed in the middle of the floor, dancers flowing around them.

She shook her head. Feeling like Cinderella at the ball, with the clock ticking, she took his hand and led him toward the door of the Longhorn.

Chapter Seven

Taylor's RV was in the crowded park at the rodeo grounds on the edge of town. It had seen better days, but he probably didn't make much money. He'd reached the RV before her, and unlocked the door.

"Wait. How do you get your RV up here, and have Angelina's trailer and the truck?" she asked as she climbed out of her car.

"A friend drops off the RV for me." He pushed open the door and motioned for her to enter ahead of him.

The place was clean, though a little shabby. Had he cleaned knowing he would bring her back here tonight? That he might have been anticipating as much as she was sent a thrill through her.

"What friend? Someone you work with?"

"Yep." He closed and locked the door behind him.

The RV suddenly seemed a lot smaller. She backed up till she bumped into the counter. "Why don't you stay in the motel? Wouldn't that be easier? And more comfortable?"

"This is cheaper."

She dropped her gaze. She shouldn't have let him buy her

those drinks. "Oh." Maybe that meant he didn't bring many girls back here. Though, look at him. He was beautiful. He was never lonely unless he wanted to be. "I haven't done this in a long time. I mean, this isn't something I do."

"I know." He cupped his hand over her jaw, lifting her face. "I'm no saint, Lavender."

Her heart plummeted. Next week he'd be at another rodeo, would have another woman in his arms. Isn't that what he was telling her? Could she expect more? "Okay," was all she could manage.

He rubbed his thumb over the curve of her cheek. "But it's been a while for me, too. And tonight, it's just you and me."

His kiss was different, deeper, hungrier, goal-oriented. She slid her hands up his arms, stroking over his biceps, closing over his shoulders as he slid his fingers along the waistband of her jeans, slipping them under the hem of her blouse, over the sensitive skin of her waist.

His mouth abandoned hers to slide along her jaw, back to that place below her ear where he'd kissed her earlier. His fingertips were rough on her skin and she imagined that touch everywhere. The sensations that shot out from his touch nearly sent her to her knees. As if he sensed it, he pressed his hips a little harder against hers, pinning her to the counter. She gasped his name and he lifted his head. Time stood still for a moment while he looked at her, then she closed her hands over the opening of his shirt.

"There's something I've been wanting to do since I met you," she said. "Can I?"

"Can you what?"

She tugged his shirt in opposite directions, but instead of the ripple of unsnapping buttons, she heard the ripping of fabric.

He stepped back and stared at his shredded shirt. The snaps of his shirt had held stronger than the soft fabric, which now hung in tatters on either side of his placket, baring his hard-muscled bare chest.

Lavender raised her hand to her mouth and her eyes to his. "I'm so sorry! I thought it would just unsnap! I'll buy you a new one."

The glint in his eyes promised retribution. A thrill sparked her blood and she edged away from him, sliding free and bolting toward the back of the trailer, and presumably, the bedroom. She squealed when he chased her, caught her around the waist and fell with her to the bed.

"Turnabout's fair play."

She squirmed underneath him, making his eyes go dark again. "No, please don't! I love this blouse."

He slid his hands from the hem to the waist of her jeans.

"And these jeans. Please, don't, Taylor."

He slipped his fingers under the waistband and found the silky fabric of her panties. He lifted his eyebrows in question. "No, no! These are the only sexy panties I have, and you know there's no place to get them here in Cascade!"

"Sexy, hm?" He rubbed the fabric between his fingers.

"Well, as in, not cotton."

"This I have to see for myself."

He pulled her upright and stripped her blouse over her head as she pushed his ruined shirt from his shoulders. His eyes glinted at the sight of her full breasts in her best black lace bra and he dragged his mouth from the underside of her chin, down her throat and over the curves, pressing kisses between them, lifting them in his hands, his thumbs sliding over her nipples. Heat shot straight to her core at the caress, then he closed his mouth over one lace-clad nipple, drawing it into his mouth, hot and eager, suckling, then abandoning it for the other.

Just when she slid her hand up to close over the back of his head to hold him to her, he lifted his head and reached for the waistband of her jeans. She returned the favor, tugging his belt open, then diving for his button fly.

"Can I trust you?" he asked solemnly, dropping to his side facing her.

"I told you it's been awhile. I may be a little overeager."

"I like overeager." He let her skim his jeans down his legs and started peeling hers, panties and all.

So much for picking her sexy underwear.

But he made her feel so good, not self-conscious at all, as she'd feared. He made her laugh, and he made her ache, and then he made her come, his fingers quick and skilled, and he dragged out the sensation before she begged him to fill her. He reached across the bed to fumble in a drawer with one hand while he unhooked her bra with the other. The rustle of cellophane filled the tiny room as he nuzzled her breast, suckling, stroking. She reached between them for his erection and he gasped against her skin when she closed her fingers around him, stroked slowly, learning him, learning what pleased him. Which seemed to be everything, judging by his breathing.

He lifted his head and pressed the open condom into her hand. "Don't rip this, too."

"Why? Aren't there more?"

"There's more."

"Thank God," she murmured, and sheathed him. Then she parted for him and cried out as he filled her slowly, slowly, waiting for her body to accept him before he started moving. He cradled her face in his hands and looked at her when he started to move.

Then she was moving too, and they found a rhythm, only to lose it and find another, then another.

"I'm fine if you want to lead this time," he teased.

"I don't remember how."

He withdrew and rolled onto his back, reaching for her.

"You'll figure it out."

Never would she have thought she would have the confidence to be on top, not with a young, handsome cowboy. How had he managed to melt her resistance, her self-consciousness? But this wasn't just a young, handsome cowboy. This was Taylor, and she brought him into her, dragging a moan from both of them. He didn't touch her until she found a rhythm that suited both of them, then he closed his hands over her hips and surged into her, matching her movements.

"I don't think I can—"

"Oh, yes, you can." And he dipped his thumb between them, dragging it along that bundle of nerves and bringing her to a shattering orgasm before tumbling her onto her back and driving into her, finding his own pleasure before collapsing over her.

~

"I HATE SENDING YOU HOME."

Taylor lay on his side, one hand propped under his head as he watched Lavender gather her scattered clothes and put them on again.

She was still shaking from their second go-round, and knew if she didn't leave now, she wouldn't. And boy, wouldn't that cause all kinds of problems.

"I hate leaving," she murmured, afraid to look at him. "What time are you heading out tomorrow?"

"Early."

A lump formed in her throat. "So I won't see you again."

"I'll be back in three weeks."

She made herself turn to him then. "I don't need promises."

But God, she wanted them.

"Lavender." He rolled to his feet, pulled on his jeans without his jockeys, and reached for her.

She let him pull her close, tucked her head under his chin.

"I'm not kidding myself about what this is. I know there's not a future."

"But it doesn't have to already be the past, either. I'll be back in three weeks. I'll want to see you."

She eased back and placed her fingers over his lips. She'd heard it all before. "No promises, Taylor, okay? Thank you." She pulled out of his arms, hating how empty she felt without him wrapped around her. "This is the most fun I've had in ages. The whole weekend, not just tonight. Thank you." And before she could start bawling, she hurried out the door.

She wondered how debauched she looked when she came in the front door of the house. Just when she was about to reassure herself that her grandmother wouldn't see her until the morning–well, later in the morning–she heard raised voices coming from the kitchen.

"Mrs. Aguilar?" she asked, rounding the corner.

And stopped short to see a strange woman facing off with Gertrude.

Okay, not strange, just unexpected.

"Mother? What are you doing here?"

Eleanor Prouty turned to look at her daughter, her expression softening from the mutinous look she'd given her mother. "Lavender! Have you been out?"

Out, and she smelled like Taylor. Oops. She didn't duck fast enough and Eleanor enveloped her in her arms. Lavender did not return the embrace, and Eleanor withdrew, nostrils flared just enough to tell Lavender she knew what had gone on that night.

Refusing to be ashamed, Lavender crossed the room to the refrigerator with a glance at her grandmother. Gertrude was pale, her face set stubbornly, her eyes trained on her daughter. Wishing for a beer, instead Lavender pulled out a pitcher of water and poured herself a glass with shaking hands before turning to face her mother.

"What are you doing here?" she repeated.

"I didn't think I needed an invitation to my own home."

"This hasn't been your home for awhile. And why come in the middle of the night? How long has it been?"

She didn't have to ask. She knew to the day–four years, three months, a week and four days. She just wondered if Eleanor was aware.

"Too long." Eleanor tried for a soothing tone but it had no effect on Lavender.

"Are you hiding from someone? Or just running away again?"

Eleanor's expression hardened into a replica of Gertrude's. "You are just like your grandmother."

Lavender bit back the desire to say she wouldn't be if Eleanor hadn't abandoned her to care for Gertrude all these years, but that would only hurt her grandmother, and she couldn't do that.

She took inventory of her mother. Eleanor looked worn out, her long hair graying from roots to ears, exhaustion dragging at her face. She'd gained weight, so the gypsy skirt she wore stretched over her hips, and her battered sandals displayed equally battered feet. What had her mother been doing the past four years? Did she really want to know, or did that give her mother too much power?

"I just came to see the two of you, see how you were doing."
"We're fine. Does that mean you'll leave now?"

Her mother sighed. "Why do you hate me so much?"

"I don't hate you. I don't feel anything for you. You are nothing to me." Liar, liar, liar. She didn't hate her mother, that was true. But seeing her raised all kinds of hope, hope she hadn't let herself experience in four years. And in two years before that. And five years before that. She took a deep breath. "How long are you staying this time?"

"As long as you'll have me."

Lavender buried the hope those words raised. Hope that she could visit Taylor in Alpine, hope that she could move forward with her life, give some of her responsibilities over to her mother.

She set the glass down on the counter. "Well. The sheets on your bed haven't been changed in awhile, but otherwise the room is ready. Church is at nine." Lavender crossed the room to kiss her grandmother's cheek, nodded to her mother, and headed up the stairs.

LAVENDER DROPPED into the pew at church the next morning. Eleanor's sudden appearance had one benefit. She commandeered the gossip that would have focused on Lavender and her behavior at the Longhorn last night. She had no illusions her actions would remain secret from Gertrude, but she was grateful for the reprieve.

Eleanor made her way to the seat beside her and Lavender struggled to balance her emotions. The little girl in her was excited to see her mother, more a fun relative than parent. Another part of her also held a childlike hope that her mother would step in, take over her own responsibilities, freeing Lavender.

For what? To chase Taylor to Alpine? She wouldn't do that, even if she could.

Who was she kidding? They'd had one night, that was it.

No telling if he ever wanted to see her again, if he even had told the truth about wanting her to come to Alpine.

Still lost in her own thoughts after the service, Lavender wandered out of church with vague greetings to her neighbors and the minister. Her focus sharpened on a white horse trailer hitched to a battered blue Ford pick-up. And the long, lean cowboy with his arms folded over his chest, leaning against the fender. Her heart kicked hard, but she schooled her steps, excusing herself from her mother and grandmother to cross the lot toward him.

He'd had his gaze on her since she walked out of the church but he only straightened when she was a car length away. She wanted to throw herself against him but was too aware of the entire town no doubt watching. His eyes flicked behind her, confirming her suspicions.

"I thought you'd be on the road already," she said, stopping a few feet away, close enough to smell him but not close enough to be tempted to touch.

"I thought you might want to say goodbye to Angelina." He inclined his head toward the far side of the trailer, away from the curious eyes of the congregation.

"Yes, I would," she murmured, her pulse picking up as she followed him.

Once they were out of sight, he spun and caught her in a fluid move, scooping his hand under her hair and covering her mouth with his. Only a moment passed before she overcame her surprise and parted her lips, sliding her palms across his shoulders, pressing against him, wanting the feel of him against her.

"I wanted to say goodbye," he said, easing back just enough to look into her eyes, his fingers still threading through her hair.

She tilted her head and smiled. "You said goodbye last night."

"That was last night."

"How did you know where to find me?"

"I checked each of the churches until I saw your car." He inclined his head toward her Toyota.

Surprise and pleasure bubbled up in her. She hadn't even realized he knew her car. They'd only known each other three days. "Who's that with Gertrude?"

She followed his gaze between the truck and the trailer to where Eleanor stood on the steps, in the same clothes she'd been wearing last night. Lavender hadn't seen her bring in any luggage, but then, Lavender had other things on her mind.

"My mother showed up last night."

He raised his eyebrows. "Not good news?"

She sighed. "That remains to be seen. Usually, no."

He stroked his fingers down her cheek and kissed her again, slowly, regretfully. "I've got to go. I'll be back in three weeks."

He released her and backed toward the cab of his truck. She folded her arms in front of her and watched as he drove off with a wave out the driver's side window.

And then he was gone and she was left to face the congregation, all lined on the sidewalk, watching.

Chapter Eight

"You DID GET in late last night," Gertrude chided when the three women filed into the house after a silent ride from church.

Lavender rubbed a hand over her stomach as if that would relieve the tension tightening it. "You didn't notice last night?" She was determined to remain casual as she walked to the fridge for eggs and sausage.

"I didn't realize you'd been making a fool of yourself with a rodeo cowboy."

Lavender bent to retrieve the cast iron skillet from the cabinet beneath the stove, struggling to find words to defend herself. Heck, why should she have to defend herself? "Why shouldn't I have some fun?"

"Having fun is one thing, but making yourself an idiot over a man is something else." Gertrude gave her daughter a pointed look, which Eleanor ignored as she spooned coffee into the filter. "Has he promised he'll be back?"

This time, Lavender glanced at her mother. "I know better than to believe those promises."

"It's different with a man, when sex is involved," Gertrude

said in the most matter-of-fact tone Lavender had ever heard her use.

Lavender's face heated. She did not want to discuss sex with her mother and grandmother. She never had in the past and didn't want to start now, with the memory of Taylor's touch so fresh.

"Do you want breakfast or not?" Lavender clanged the pan against the burners. "I have a right to a life, to not being lonely, okay? I deserve to be held, to be touched, to feel beautiful and wanted. And if I never see him again, if he never comes back, I have how he made me feel last night."

Gertrude sat at the table, her jaw set. "You've already been hurt so much."

"No one has that power anymore." But even as she said it to the two women who stared at her, she knew it wasn't true. Taylor had already breached her defenses.

Taylor pulled his truck up in the circular drive in front of his ranch house, shut off the ignition and just sat.

He'd never had a hard time leaving an event, never spent an entire drive thinking about the woman he left behind.

What was different about Lavender?

Her acceptance of him, for one thing. After her initial reluctance to get to know him, she hadn't cared that he was a rodeo rider, didn't know about his former life, just accepted him for who he was.

That made it easy to be with her, to tease her, to coax out that pretty smile, that fun personality that seemed to be buried under all those layers of loneliness.

He looked through the dirty windshield at the mountains edging his ranch, framing his dream house.

His empty dream house. God, he knew what loneliness was.

He pulled the door handle and shoved his shoulder against the truck door. It creaked open and his housekeeper appeared on the wraparound porch, wiping her hands on her jeans, glancing at the truck in alarm. He didn't usually park this truck up here, usually left it at the stables with the trailer, but he had been too weary to walk up from the stables.

"Mr. Creighton?" She used his real name, not his alias. "Are you all right? We were getting worried. Are you hungry? Dinner will be in a couple of hours, but if you need-"

He held up a hand to stop the flow of words and hefted his bag onto his shoulder. "I'll just get a sandwich or something later, Mrs. Bennigan. Don't go to any trouble."

Her lips tightened in disapproval, reminding him of Gertrude. "It's what you pay me for." She reached for his duffle.

He relinquished it reluctantly. What would she think of the shirt Lavender had shredded? She'd probably throw it away and think he was a man-whore. At the last minute, he closed his hand around the strap.

"There's a few things I need out of here."

"I'll bring them to you."

"I'll just toss the clothes in the hamper." He shifted the duffle back onto his shoulder.

"Mr. Creighton? Is something wrong? Are you feeling all right?"

"I'm good." But he stopped and looked over what passed for a front lawn. "Do you think roses would grow out here?"

"I figured it out!"

Jerri burst into Lavender's classroom after the morning announcements, waving a magazine.

Lavender looked up, startled, from tying Bethany's shoe. "What?" She straightened, her focus on the magazine.

"I knew I'd seen your cowboy somewhere." Jerri jabbed a finger at the picture.

Lavender took the teen magazine. And there, in the middle of five young men known as Crushin', Taylor Craig smiled up at her, with a very white, very fake smile.

"He was in a boy band!" Jerri blurted, as if Lavender couldn't see the page in front of her. "I'd seen an interview not too long ago on one of those entertainment shows, you know, and they were talking about how Crushin' was going to get back together and they showed Taylor's picture and said he couldn't be reached. He's the only hold-out, I think. They're going back on tour, can you believe it?"

Lavender lowered herself slowly to the edge of one of the tables, oblivious to the children, only staring at the fake Taylor smile. Taylor Creighton was the name he went by then. He'd liked romantic dinners on the beach, mint chocolate chip ice cream and girls who had the natural look.

Naturally. She dragged her hand through her hair.

Taylor Creighton was in Crushin'. Well. That explained his sense of rhythm.

The noise level in her class brought her out of her shock, and she called them together for a math lesson, trying to put the picture out of her head.

But as soon as the class went out for PE, she hunkered down in front of her computer and started Googling.

Many of the sites were blocked by her district's filtering system, but she was able to discover that Taylor Creighton was twenty-seven now, twenty when he'd been in the boy band, so baby-faced, so slender. And wow, had he made bad fashion choices. Yeesh.

How had he gone from singing songs like "Love Me 'Til the

End of Time" and "Goin' Crazy Tonight" – obnoxious earworms, both of them – to wrestling steers in a small town rodeo?

And why was he working...?

. Of course, he wasn't working on a ranch. He didn't sleep in a bunkhouse, despite that battered truck and old RV. Her heart sank inexplicably when she realized her fantasy had only been, well, a fantasy. Instead of working on a ranch, no doubt he owned it.

Everything she thought she knew about him was wrong. She couldn't even say he'd lied to her because he hadn't told her anything. He'd neatly deflected any conversation that headed that way.

When they had talked.

She closed out the window and sat back on her rolling chair. Gertrude was right in more ways than she knew. Lavender had been a complete idiot over Taylor Creighton.

When she went home, though, she couldn't stay away from the computer, looking up old videos – the boy could dance – buying a couple of downloaded songs and trying to pick out his voice, that same low voice even at his young age.

She even found a couple of videos of interviews. His manner- isms were so different, so big and effusive. If not for the glint in his eyes, she wouldn't have believed Jerri.

The band broke up six years ago and Lavender couldn't find any information on Taylor Creighton after that, until speculation ran rampant the past few months, everything from whether he'd died in some horrible manner to wondering if he'd become a woman. Definitely not that.

She Googled Taylor Craig, and the first thing she could find on him was last year. What had happened in the intervening years?

She searched for more lurid information – scandals, gossip,

anything that would explain why the band broke up. But any information was buried.

Why this discovery hurt, she couldn't say. Clearly he didn't want anyone to make the connection or he wouldn't have changed his name. It wasn't personal.

But nothing about this relationship was personal, was it?

She shut off the computer, climbed into bed and cried herself to sleep.

SHE BUSIED herself with end of school activities – field day, field trips, kindergarten graduation. She didn't go back to the rodeo or the Longhorn, but she did continue dance lessons with Samantha. She couldn't believe she'd tried to dance with a member of Crushin'.

She didn't think of Taylor more than a dozen times a day.

She was back in her life. This was where she belonged, not in a romance, in a relationship, in a cowboy's bed.

But summer loomed. Empty. Scary. Lonely.

Eleanor hadn't taken off yet, and finding her at the breakfast table was less of a surprise every morning. Lavender had to guard herself against complacency, because she knew that the moment she weakened and let her mother back into her heart – bam.

As it was, Eleanor worked at becoming for a part in their lives, wanting to run Gertrude on errands, but Lavender blocked her as often as possible. She saw her grandmother softening toward Eleanor and worried that Gertrude would be the one hurt this time.

At least Eleanor had let Samantha fix those awful gray roots and even out the ends of her hair, though Eleanor protested the loss of the length. Gertrude bought her new sandals and blouses that didn't display her large breasts quite so much. Lavender's grandmother even paid to tune up the station wagon that would take Eleanor out of their lives again.

Every day Lavender came home expecting to find Eleanor gone and Gertrude crying.

Her heart lurched the last Friday before school was out when she pulled into the driveway to find the station wagon gone. She left her purse in the car and bolted into the house. Panic tightened her chest when she could find neither Gertrude nor Eleanor. She thundered up the stairs to Eleanor's room.

Her things were still strewn about. Lavender allowed a small sigh of relief to escape and leaned against the door, trying to reason out where the women could be.

Downstairs, a door slammed open.

"Lavender, could you move your car from the driveway so we don't have to carry the groceries in from the street?" Eleanor called.

Grocery shopping. That's where they'd been. Eleanor again, trying to worm her way back into Gertrude's good graces. Taking a deep breath, Lavender headed down the stairs, ready to lay into her mother.

But Gertrude's smile brought her up short. Could she ask her grandmother not to enjoy her time with her daughter because of how it would hurt when Eleanor left? How much of a hypocrite would that make her? Gertrude deserved to be happy for the time she had with her daughter, didn't she?

So she swallowed her arguments and marched out to the car to put it in the street.

Taylor tightened his hands on the steering wheel as he pulled into the Cascade city limits. He hadn't been so anxious about seeing a woman again in–well, ever. He didn't come back to women.

But he'd been counting the days before he came back to this one. He'd even come back to Cascade two days early.

He drove Angelica to the rodeo grounds, got her settled into the stall, and headed for the school.

The parking lot was almost empty. He frowned. Hadn't she told him today was her last day of school? Where was everyone? Why hadn't he gotten her number and given her a call?

But no, there was her Toyota, at the end of the lot. He pulled in next to it and waited.

Even in the shade of the live oak, the cab of the truck heated up in the afternoon temperatures, so he got out of the truck and sat on the hood to wait.

Just when he thought he'd have to go in after her, she walked out, paused on the steps to paw through her bag, pulled out her keys and started down the steps again.

Then she saw him and stopped. Froze. He slid off the truck and waited for her to move again, to run into his arms. When she didn't, only approaching him slowly, well, he couldn't say why he was so disappointed.

She stopped in front of him and shifted her bag on her shoulder. "You're back early."

Okay, this was not the welcome he'd hoped for. Had he done something wrong? "Is that bad?"

She smiled, but it wasn't the smile he'd gotten the Saturday night before he left. He wanted that smile, and was thrown. He couldn't remember how to coax it out. Why couldn't he remember?

"I missed you." He stepped forward, wanting to touch her, to kiss her, satisfied himself with stroking a finger down her sleeve. Only that wasn't satisfying at all. He reached up to tuck her hair behind her ear, letting his fingertips touch her skin, so soft. That he remembered. He bent in for a kiss.

Then she ducked. "I had onions on my hamburger at lunch."

"I don't care." He had to taste her, wouldn't let her back away, caught her little moan with his mouth.

Yes. She parted her lips and tilted his head, welcoming him. He ran his fingertips up and down the back of her neck, just kiss- ing, tasting, remembering. But when he slid his hand down her spine to pull her closer, she broke away.

"I'm sweaty. I've been working in my room." She lifted her gaze to his, tucking her hair behind her ear. "I didn't think I'd see you today."

"Let's go somewhere." He eased back and took her hand.

She pulled her hand away. "Taylor. I'm filthy." Disappointment weighed on him. He wanted to hear her voice, hear her laugh. He wanted to touch her, kiss her.

"Okay, I'll tell you what. You go home, get cleaned up. I'll come get you in an hour."

When she still hesitated, a thought struck him.

"Did you have something else going on tonight?" She hadn't been expecting him. Did she have a date?

She smiled, still not his smile, but a softer, more relaxed one.

"No. I just imagined this differently. Me not sweaty and dirty, for one."

He smiled and curled his fingers around the back of her neck again. "You look gorgeous. And you've kissed me when I was sweaty and dirty."

She moved toward her car. "An hour and a half, okay?"

"Lavender. You don't have to be perfect for me. You know that."

"An hour and a half, okay?" she repeated, opening the car door and tossing her bag inside. Then she turned back to him, pulled his head down and kissed him hard before jumping in her car.

He grinned as she drove away.

~

AN HOUR and a half was barely enough time to do what he needed to do, and he pulled up in front of her house ten minutes late, wishing he'd had time for a shower himself.

Lavender didn't answer his knock. An older woman in a long denim skirt and a Las Vegas T-shirt did.

"Mrs. Prouty. I'm Taylor Craig." He offered his hand and resisted the urge to look past her for Lavender. Instead, he met her mother's inspection, looking for Lavender in her mother's life-worn features.

"The rodeo cowboy." Judgment colored her voice.

"Yes, ma'am." She didn't have Lavender's pretty brown eyes, or her pretty smile. He saw the shape of Lavender's face, her nose, but none of her spirit. Would Lavender become this woman if she didn't find something to keep the joy in her life?

Could he help her keep it?

The thought jolted him more than the sight of Lavender coming down the stairs, pretty in a pink scoop-necked blouse and calf length jeans, with pink sandals. He took a step toward her before he remembered her mother was in his way. So he rocked back and stayed on the porch. There was the smile he'd been waiting for, just for him, and something loosened in his chest, a tension he hadn't realized he felt.

"Ready to go?" he asked pointlessly.

She put her hand on her mother's shoulder, eased her aside. "Don't wait up."

But as Taylor took her hand, he sensed her carefree attitude was all for show. "Everything okay?" he asked.

Her fingers tightened in his. "Let's just go, okay?"

He watched her face, saw the tight lines around her mouth. He knew she had issues with her mother, but not the details. Instead of questioning her, he took the coward's way and held his truck door open.

"Where are we going?" she asked, tilting the vent toward her.

He watched the air blow her hair back from her face. She closed her eyes in appreciation and his mouth dried at the pleasure in her expression. He shifted to ease the heaviness in his groin and put the truck into drive.

"A picnic. I found the perfect place."

She turned with a smile. "Overlooking the winery?"

"Uh." So much for his surprise. "Yeah."

"There aren't that many picnic places around," she said in response to his reaction.

"Took me some time to find, once I asked the lady at the bakery for a good spot."

She slid him a look. "You went to the bakery?"

"And the Handy Andy." He nodded toward the basket in the back of the cab. "I couldn't find a regular picnic basket but they had some leftover Easter baskets. I might've overdone it. I was kinda hungry."

She smiled. "What'd you get at the bakery?"

"The lady there said you liked the brownies."

She blushed. "You told her who you were taking?"

"Should I not have?"

"Doesn't matter. You want to turn here."

He gave his attention to the road. "Huh. That's not the way I got here before."

"Trust me."

So he turned and got to the shady hilltop overlooking the winery and its fields of grapes in neat rows, in half the time as before. But when he was shaking the tablecloth out onto the ground, he could have sworn he heard her humming something familiar.

And not the song they'd danced to at the Longhorn.

A song he hoped he'd never hear again. How did she find out? He looked at her sharply. "What's that?"

She knelt at the edge of the tablecloth and blinked at him innocently. "What?"

"What you're humming."

"Sound familiar?" She unpacked the French bread, deli sliced turkey, cheese and tomatoes and a bag of chips.

He dropped onto his ass and looped his arms over his knees. "How'd you find out?"

"Jerri, the blonde from the Longhorn, recognized you." She reached in the oversized bag she'd brought and pulled out one ofthose damned teen magazines, already bent open to a page with the members of Crushin' spread across the page.

"Ah, hell."

Her eyebrows winged up over bright eyes. "You were pretty cute."

He rolled his eyes. He didn't want that complicated part of his life mixed with the pleasant simplicity of being here with her.

"Lavender, I don't want–it's not something I'm proud of."

She sank onto her bottom, her legs folded to the side as she flipped the magazine closed. "I just want to know how you went from this to, well, this."

"I don't talk about it." He picked up a bottle opener for the wine.

"Oh." She rolled up the magazine to tuck it back in her bag, but he reached for it and flung it off the hillside.

She stared, and heat crept up his own neck. But she didn't say anything, just took the knife from the basket and sliced the bread. "It was an opportunity," he blurted, stopping with the cork half out of the bottle. Okay, so he'd never hold up under torture, not when Lavender's silence made him cave. "I'd tried to get into acting, and it never went through. But some scouts saw me, approached my parents, and they signed me up."

"How old were you?"

"Fifteen."

She peered up at him, still making the sandwiches. "But not your choice."

He sighed and looked out over the open land. "At the time, I thought it would be cool. All that money, all those girls. Then I ended up being the family breadwinner, and the bread just wasn't enough, you know?"

She set down the loaf and watched him now, but didn't speak. Her silence was no longer a pressure, but an offering for him to talk. He hadn't talked to anyone about this in, well, ever. He finished opening the bottle of wine, set it aside to let it breathe, and leaned back on his hands.

"At first, you know, it was a big deal. Photographers and girls and people throwing money at us, pretty much. We didn't have to go to school, we had tutors, but no one was really strict about it. We saw all these places we'd never thought we'd see, and we had this incredible freedom.

"But the more popular we got, the less freedom we had. The less we saw, the less we could go out. It was just hotel to venue to airport, alternating with home to recording studio to dance studio, and it was exhausting, and boring."

"And you couldn't stop."

The empathy in her tone surprised him. "I couldn't stop," he repeated. "My dad had quit his job, my mom had moved the family into this huge house that we never would have been able to even drive past before I joined the band. If I quit, we would lose everything."

"You were just a kid."

"With way more earning potential than either of my parents."

"So what happened?"

He shrugged. "The inevitable. We got too old, stopped being marketable. Boy bands went out of fashion."

"And you lost everything?"

He blew a breath out his nose. "I know you hear those stories about parents mismanaging kids' money like that, but my dad was pretty smart. He knew it couldn't last forever, and he sure didn't want to go back to work. He invested it well. We did sell the house in California, though, and my parents and three younger brothers moved into a smaller, though still very nice place, and I bought my ranch."

"Why a ranch?" she asked.

He looked over at her then. That wasn't the direction he'd expected her to go, but okay. "I had a friend, an actor, who had a place out in Alpine. I went out there a few times, fell in love with it, and bought a ranch."

"And the rodeo thing?"

"It just seemed to fit. And I guess I just can't stay out of the spotlight."

"Though you managed to for six years."

"Yeah, I'd kinda missed out on the 'finding myself' years."

"Is that why you aren't planning to be a part of the reunion tour?"

He nodded. That and so much more. He was a different

person now, had nothing in common with the men he'd grown up with. Didn't want to have anything in common with them.

She passed him a sandwich he hadn't realized she'd finished constructing. "What about your parents? Do you still get along with them?"

He choked out a laugh. "Not that I ever did, much, but yeah, we can tolerate each other pretty well. They live up near Redwood City. That's far enough, I think."

"And the rodeo thing? Do they get it?"

"Not many do." He bit into his sandwich. Good. Just the right balance.

"What about the other guys? Are you still in touch with them?"

He fished a napkin out of the basket. "We were glad to get away from each other, there at the end. So, no. No friends from the old life." And not too many from the new.

"The truck, the trailer, the RV, that's all just to blend in."

"Why draw attention to myself when no one else on this circuit who scores like I do, makes the money it would take to drive a shiny new truck?" The horse trailer was in the best shape of his belongings, only because he couldn't see Angelina having to suffer because of his pride. "I want to be noticed for what I do now, not who I was."

She retrieved the wine glasses and poured, handed him a glass and saluted him with her own. "To Taylor Craig."

He clinked his glass with hers. "And new friends." But even as he drank, he wondered how many other people knew who he was.

Chapter Nine

Lavender watched the rise and fall of Taylor's chest as he slept. He sprawled on his back, one hand flung above his head, his knuckles resting on the headboard. He'd gotten a room at The Corral instead of bringing his RV, and he'd invited her to stay. While Lavender had trepidations about spending the night and being the talk of the town, she was determined to take the bull by the horns and grab what happiness she could while she could.

His confession out by the winery earlier had touched her heart. Like her, he'd been fifteen and handed a tremendous responsibility. How could she have judged him for not being responsible when he'd supported his family for five years? No wonder he was drawn to the rambling life, where he could make his own choices, make his own way, not depend on anyone else. Not have anyone else depend on him.

He was living her dream. But what did that mean to her?

He snuffled in his sleep and turned toward her, looping his arm over her waist, opening one eye sleepily when his arm encountered fabric.

"Why you wearin' my shirt?" he asked groggily.

"I got up to go to the bathroom." She nestled closer. "And the air conditioner's too cold."

He pulled her closer, so her hands were flat against his bare chest. "That's when you come back to bed and put your cold feet on my legs and wake me up." He nuzzled his mouth under her jaw. Lavender shivered. "I'll be glad to warm you up."

"Do your best," she teased, and this time, *he* ripped the shirt from *her* body.

THEY SURFACED on Thursday night to go to the Longhorn. Though they'd spent the past two days only in each other's company, in each other's arms, Lavender didn't feel particularly sociable. The place was hopping, though, with the rodeo tomorrow night, and Lavender spotted the other teachers sitting at a table by the dance floor, waving.

She headed toward them but Taylor tugged her hand, tucking her back against his side before pressing a kiss to her temple.

"Where are you going?"

"To say hi." She inclined her head toward the three women. "Just for a minute. Don't want to share you tonight."

She turned to slide her hand around his waist, well aware of the attention on them, probably wondering what old maid Lavender was doing with hottie Taylor Craig. Well, if they looked closely, they could reason it out.

She pushed the thoughts aside. She wouldn't ruin her mood by speculating. "We're in the wrong place for that."

"Go say hi to your friends. I'll get us something to drink." He kissed her forehead and slid free of her embrace.

She watched after him for a minute—he looked good coming and going—before she headed to the table by the dance floor.

"Lavender, you look amazing," Melissa greeted her. "Love agrees with you."

Lavender's face heated even as Jerri leaned back to inspect her through narrowed eyes.

"You mean sex agrees with her. Those younger guys are certainly attentive, aren't they?"

Yeowch. Now, there was no call for that. Lavender knew Taylor wasn't in love with her, didn't pretend otherwise. But she was determined to maintain her good mood. "I don't know. I don't have much in the way of comparison."

"Now you will." Melissa's gaze followed Taylor wistfully. "Is it true he was in Crushin'? I had the biggest thing for Ronny from that group. Do you think Taylor could introduce me?"

"He doesn't have much to do with them anymore." Lavender wanted to end this conversation before he got back. "It was another life."

Jerri widened her eyes mockingly. "So you do have actual conversations?"

Okay, what was her problem? Jealousy, maybe. Jerri was younger, slimmer, prettier than Lavender. Maybe she thought she deserved Taylor. Lavender took a deep breath and squared her shoulders to battle back the anger. Why couldn't the other woman allow her this one happiness?

"Well, you know, there's only so much, 'Yes! Oh, yes, Taylor, right there!' and 'Rip my clothes off with your teeth!' before, you know, you have to find something else to talk about."

She pivoted and came face to face with Taylor, a smile quirking the corner of his mouth, two bottles of beer dangling from his fingers. Her face flamed. How much had he heard? Had he seen her lose her temper? Okay, the lift of his eyebrows told her he'd heard enough, and damn it, he was amused. He stepped closer, offered a bottle to her, then took her hand to lead her to the dance floor.

Her earlier clumsiness returned as he shifted her into his arms and she couldn't meet his gaze. But the problem was, she couldn't look at anyone else. Who else had heard her snap?

Taylor dipped his head so his lips were next to her ear. "I think it was more like, 'Don't stop, Taylor, please God, don't stop'."

Relief at his teasing swept away some of the embarrassment. She eased back a bit to shove playfully at a shoulder. "I just made a complete idiot of myself."

"I like a woman who can stand up for herself." He looped a lock of her hair over her ear, let his fingertips linger on her cheek. "I was getting ready to jump in."

"That would have made it worse." If that was possible.

"Nah, you did good. Turned it back on yourself, but made it funny. It'll be a joke for a bit, and then it will blow over."

She didn't want to think about the gossip that would result. Even if no one heard, well, Jerri had a big mouth. "Don't."

He grinned, all white teeth. "Don't stop, you mean?"

"Taylor."

He rested his hand holding the beer on the small of her back as they moved across the floor. "I want to hear more about ripping your clothes off with my teeth. I wonder if that's possible. Let's go find out."

"COME BACK TO ALPINE WITH ME."

Lavender whipped her head up so fast she almost cracked him in the jaw as they snuggled in bed. She couldn't get enough of touching him, and lying in bed with her legs linked around his was one of her favorite new things. She loved the rasp of his hair against her sensitive skin and had been concentrating on that when he dropped his bombshell.

When she met his gaze, he smiled and threaded his fingers through her hair. "I want you to see where I live. And I'm not ready to be away from you yet."

"Taylor, even if I wanted to, my grandmother—"

"Eleanor's been doing a fine job of taking care of her these past few days. You said so yourself."

She bit her lower lip and looked down. He tucked his finger under her chin and lifted her face.

"Why do you feel like you have to carry the weight of the world?"

"You know why. If anyone knows, you do. If I don't, who will?"

"She's stayed longer than you thought she would."

She had. Lavender wasn't sure why, but her mother's visit this time had surpassed the length of any since Lavender was fifteen. Still, with her luck, Eleanor would leave while Lavender was in Alpine.

"I want you to see my house." He stroked his thumb over her cheek. "It would mean a lot to me. I even planted some roses."

Everything in her melted, and she nestled closer. "You did?"

"Reminded me of you," he murmured, and kissed her again. The knock came at the door just as Lavender was dozing off,

Taylor's arm across her waist, his body curved around hers. She jolted at the sound and woke him.

"What?" he asked, rolling onto his back and rubbing his eyes. "Someone's at the door."

"What time is it?"

She glanced at the clock. "Not midnight yet."

Her words were almost drowned by another knock, stronger

this time, accompanied by, "Lavender Prouty! Are you in there?"

A man's voice. Fear took over as Lavender twisted to look at Taylor. "Something might have happened to Gertrude or my mother."

"Who is it?" he asked her, rolling out of bed and grabbing his jeans.

"I don't know." She reached over the edge of the bed for his shirt, slipped it on and snapped it as he approached the door and peered out through the peephole.

He looked back at her. "It's Mr. Hendrickson from the front desk. You okay?"

She stood and tugged the tail of his shirt down, then folded her arms and nodded. Taylor opened the door.

"Mr. Hendrickson. How can I help you this evening?"

Before the words were out of his mouth, cameras flashed out of nowhere. He ducked his head, pushing Lavender behind him as the questions rolled through the night.

"Taylor, where have you been the past six years? Who is this woman?"

"Taylor, how did you end up in Texas? In a rodeo?"

"Taylor, are you going to join the Crushin' reunion tour?"

Mr. Hendrickson was shoved aside by the reporters who lunged toward Taylor. Out of practice after six years, he didn't get the door shut before they got a few more pictures but no answers. With his shoulder against the closed door, he turned his accusing gaze to Lavender.

"Where did they come from?"

She widened her eyes. "You think I called them?"

He sagged against the door, glanced toward the window and blew a breath out through his nose. "No. No, I know you didn't. Jesus, though. Where did they come from? And why?"

Another pounding at the door made him jolt, then throw the privacy lock.

But it was Mrs. Hendrickson's voice that came through the door. "Lavender, honey, you have a phone call in the office. It's Mrs. Aguilar. She said come quick. Your mama's gone again."

LAVENDER HURRIED up the walk to the house, tucking Taylor's shirt into her jeans. Behind her, Taylor sat in his truck, waiting for her to get inside, but she couldn't worry about that now. She pushed open the door to see Mrs. Aguilar pacing in the hallway, squeezing her hands together. Her face sagged in relief and she hurried forward when she saw Lavender.

"Thank goodness. Your grandmother is beside herself." She flicked a questioning gaze to the plaid western shirt, then back to Lavender's face.

"Where is she?" Lavender asked.

"In her room."

"Thank you, Mrs. Aguilar. I appreciate you being here." But her focus was already on her grandmother and what she would say to reassure her.

Was there anything to say? What would she want to hear? Certainly nothing like the I-told-you-so that was on the tip of her tongue.

She mounted the stairs and tapped on Gertrude's bedroom door. A grumble was her response.

Lavender pushed open the door to see Gertrude swiping at her eyes, though when she glared at Lavender, her eyes were watery and pained.

Lavender's heart tightened. She couldn't think of anything to say except, "She's gone?"

Instead of more tears, Gertrude glared. "Thanks to you."

Lavender hesitated. "What do you mean?"

"She came here in good faith. She wanted to make amends. But you poked at her and poked at her and poked at her and she's gone. You are an ungrateful child."

Lavender's mouth dropped open and all her good intentions fled. "Ungrateful? How long has it been since we've seen her? Heard from her? And I'm ungrateful?"

"People make mistakes. She was trying to make up to us."

"How? How was she making up?" God, she didn't want to have this fight with her grandmother, who was so hurt. She wanted to hug and comfort her, but Gertrude had all her quills out, wanting to strike out, and her only other target had fled.

Gertrude narrowed her eyes. "You haven't even been around the past few days. Your mother has helped me, taken me to the grocery store, taken me to get my hair done, taken me to the bank—"

Lavender's heart sank. "Where you gave her how much money?"

"She said she needed new tires." Gertrude lowered her head to her hands as she realized what she'd done.

Lavender dropped to her knees in front of her grandmother and wrapped her arms around the older woman, blocking her own pain. She'd known this day would come, and had thought she'd prepared for it.

She hadn't.

TAYLOR HAD FORGOTTEN how hard it was to get anything done with the media around. Back when he'd been in the band, he'd had handlers to run interference. Now he had to rely on his own wits, dulled by time. The damned reunion tour made it worse.

Otherwise, who would care? But because he'd been the hold-out from the tour, reporters wanted to know why.

Taylor was in no mood to give them answers.

He'd lost his temper only once, when they'd spooked Angelina at the rodeo grounds. Worse, the presence of the photographers and reporters—it had started at four, then six, once word got back to Los Angeles—had drawn the attention of the townspeople and the disdain of the other cowboys. He hadn't formed enough bonds to depend on their support, especially once they discovered why he was suddenly so popular. The names they called him were ones he hadn't been called in a long time.

He'd escaped with the help of Alex, his hazer, and made it to Angelina's stall before the rodeo started. He cinched Angelina's saddle and looked up when Lavender popped her head over the top of the stall. His surprise morphed quickly to joy. He had missed her last night after she left. He hadn't thought it possible, but God, he missed the smell of her, the feel of her.

A moment passed before he recognized that her eyes were shadowed and the smile she gave him was a ghost of her normal one. His gut twisted to see her in pain. He slid a hand along Angelina's neck and approached, offering her what he hoped was an understanding smile of his own.

"You okay?" He reached to touch her jaw, but she turned her head, and his stomach dropped. "That bad?" His voice sounded strained to his own ears.

"I won't be watching you ride today."

"I figured. I wish you could, but I can manage without the good luck you bring." He tugged open the stall door and caught her wrist, wanting to bring her to him, wanting to make her look at him. She hadn't since she approached, and that alone set off all sorts of warning bells. "I'll come by after."

"No." She looked at him then, pain clouding her eyes. "No, don't."

"Gertrude is still pissed at me?"

"At everyone at the moment." She sucked in a deep breath and her nose wrinkled just a bit at the smell, which was not at all rose-like. "I don't–I think you should just go on to Alpine after the rodeo."

"Okay," he said slowly. "I'll come back and get you in, what do you think, a week?" Because, damn it, she wasn't saying what he thought she was saying. Not Lavender, the woman he wanted by his side, not when he needed her.

Her nose pinched as she drew in a deep breath and looked away again. "No. I'm not going to be able to go to Alpine with you."

"Sure, until you can find someone to stay with Gertrude. Hell, bring her with you. I don't care. It's a big house."

Tears slid down her cheeks and she broke her wrist out of his grip. "I can't do this anymore. Don't you hear what I'm saying to you? It's been fun while it lasted, but it's over. I have to get back to my life, before it's too late. I'm sorry, Taylor."

She didn't give him a chance to say anything, but turned and strode back through the barn. He had the presence of mind to snick the lock on Angelina's stall before he ran after her.

"Lavender! Damn it, Lavender!"

He grabbed her arm just before she left the barn. She turned to him, full-on crying, her nose red, her eyes flashing.

"Lavender, what the hell?"

"I can't do this," she choked out and wrenched her arm free as flashes went off around them.

Too late, damn it, he saw the reporters outside the barn, all focused on him.

"I'm sorry," she murmured, and slipped through the reporters, who closed behind her, blocking his path. When he pushed through them, ignoring their shouted questions and the flashing lights, Lavender had disappeared.

"Craig! You're up!"

He wanted to ignore the summons, wanted to go after Lavender. But she was so wound up, would she listen to him? Would he even know what to say?

Blowing out a breath, he jammed his hands on his hips, then pivoted to get Angelina. At least there was one female he understood.

Or, maybe not. Just a few seconds later, Taylor lay in the dirt and stared at the fluttering colored flags on the roof of the Cascade Rodeo. Timing was everything and when he'd jumped from Angelina, he'd missed the calf and landed on his ass. Flashes went off and he closed his eyes. Great. Just great.

Taylor slammed the shot glass down on the counter, upside down and empty. Only a couple of the reporters had followed him to the Longhorn, the others had hopefully given up. These two were likely taking note of the empty glasses and his increasingly drunken state, something he'd been cautious about back in the day. But he could care less what they thought of him now.

If only he could reason out why Lavender had a change of heart. Well, he thought he knew why—she was tied here with her grandmother, but hell, the old lady was well enough to travel. For God's sake, Taylor wasn't trying to separate the two, abandon the old woman. He had gone to the house after the rodeo to reason with Lavender and she hadn't even answered the door.

He'd never taken her for a coward.

He scowled over his shoulder at the reporters. Maybe that's

who had made her run, those scavengers who'd shown up at their motel room. Maybe they'd chased her away.

He probed the floor with the toe of his boot, making sure it was still where he thought it was, and stood, body tense, ready for a fight.

A soft hand slid across his shoulder and he turned to look into familiar green eyes.

"Hey, cowboy, want to dance?" Samantha asked.

Taylor swayed for a minute, trying to remember if he'd ever seen Samantha ask anyone to dance. He couldn't recall. And hell, he was in no shape to dance with her.

She tucked an arm around his chest to turn him, then guided him to the floor.

"Samantha," he protested with a shake of his head that made his stomach roil.

"Where's our girl?" Samantha asked once she propped him up on the dance floor and slipped into his arms.

"Home with her granny." Way to keep the bitterness out of his voice.

Samantha sighed and swayed in the semblance of a dance. "I heard Eleanor took off again."

That gave him a jolt. Was that why she'd bolted? No, it couldn't be. She'd talked about "when" Eleanor left, not "if." "I don't think it was too much of a surprise to Lavender."

"It wouldn't be. Eleanor left for the first time when Lavender was fifteen. She's been back off and on, but never this long."

"Where's her dad? She never said."

"That's why Eleanor took off the first time, to find him. But Gertrude had just had her stroke, and Lavender was left alone to care for her."

"When she was fifteen." Jesus. She'd had to grow up fast, too. "So our girl has some abandonment issues."

Taylor stiffened. "I haven't abandoned her."

"Yet."

He stopped even pretending to dance, dropped his hands away. "That's why she broke off with me? So I wouldn't break off with her first?"

"I don't know, Taylor. I just know she's hurting right now, and I know she cares for you. I wanted you to understand what she's going through, and feel sorry for her instead of feeling sorry for yourself."

With that, she spun away and abandoned him on the dance floor.

Chapter Ten

Lavender wouldn't have known about her pictures in the tabloids if Eleanor hadn't refused to buy Gertrude coffee. So Lavender found herself in line at the Handy

Andy staring a lonely copy of a newspaper print tabloid with a picture of her in Taylor's room, wearing Taylor's shirt. The headline read, "Taylor's Tubby Texan."

Well, add insult to injury, why not?

The night in Taylor's hotel room, the reporters, all came back in a rush. She hadn't even considered the consequences of that, she'd been so wrapped up in her mother's abandonment. But before she could inspect the detail further, a hand yanked that last copy from the wire rack and Lavender looked into the guilty eyes of Jerri Kidwell.

Okay, maybe she would have found out sooner rather than later.

"I wanted to get it off the rack before anyone else saw it," Jerri lied quickly.

Lavender ignored her and turned to Pam, the checker. "Are there any more copies?"

"No, dear, we sold out in just a matter of hours. I could see about ordering some more, if you like."

"Right. To add to my scrapbook."

Pam beamed. "Exactly!"

"I don't think so." Lavender backed out of the store, heartsick.

So everyone in town had a copy of her shame but her.

She drove home-without the coffee, damn it–in a blur. What would the repercussions of this be? How long would they last? Could she lose her job? Her heart plummeted at the thought. If she lost her job, how could she support herself and Gertrude? The house was paid for but it was old and the upkeep was almost as much as a mortgage.

She dragged herself into the kitchen of the house she loved, toward the living room where she would tell Gertrude that she hadn't gotten the coffee though she wouldn't tell her why.

She'd barely reached the hallway when the doorbell rang.

Her mind elsewhere, Lavender wearily swept her hair back from her face and didn't think before twisting the knob and swinging it open.

"Lavender Prouty? Taylor Creighton's lover?"

If she'd looked through the beveled glass first, she would have known this young man didn't belong in Cascade, not with his suit and tie and the spiky haircut. And he moved quick, angling his body between the doorjamb and the door, gambling that her mood wasn't foul enough to hurt him.

"Not his lover," she said wearily.

The young man's expressive mouth turned down in exaggerated skepticism. "If I'm not mistaken, you spent almost a week with him in his motel room." He whipped out a copy of the tabloid, trailing his fingers down her bare legs in the photograph.

She shuddered at the motion. "It was nowhere near serious."

Expressive Boy rolled his eyes. "Of course it wasn't. He's Taylor Creighton and he's never given a girl more than a week. Honestly. But I was hoping that you might be able to give us more insight on Taylor and where he's been these past six years."

"Not interested." She slipped behind the door to close it, thinking he would move out of the way.

Wrong. He jittered even closer. "I'm Evan Zander with Celebrities Tonight. It would be an exclusive interview and we would pay you serious bucks."

Lavender frowned. "What do you want to know? I mean, he's not famous anymore."

Evan cocked his head. "Don't you just love those 'Where Are They Now?' stories? We pay very well, especially since the rest of the band is getting together now and could use the publicity. The more details you can share, the better. Based on this picture," He tapped the picture. "You have a lot of details."

Lavender blushed and glanced over her shoulder, hoping her grandmother didn't hear.

"Fifty thousand dollars, Lavender, sweetie. You could blow this joint."

She cocked a hip. "Fifty thousand dollars to tell you about Taylor Creighton. Why would I do that?"

He rolled his head as if trying to find Taylor somewhere in the vicinity. "Because he left you, babe. And payback can be a bitch."

"But I'm not." As politely as she could manage, she pushed his shoulder out of the way and closed the door, sagging against it and ignoring the little man still on the other side.

Why had she listened to her heart instead of reason? Why had she convinced herself being happy with Taylor for a few short days was worth the pain? Because it wasn't. He was gone and nothing was worth this.

TAYLOR LEANED one hand against the post on the front porch and stared out at the wilting roses he'd had planted along the driveway when he'd come back from Cascade the first time, trying to emulate Lavender's lovely garden. He should have known–he'd never nurtured anything with any success.

Certainly not Lavender.

And if anyone needed nurturing, she did. She'd spent so long taking care of other people and he'd let her kick him out without a fight.

Way to show he cared for her.

"Mr. Creighton, you have a phone call." Mrs. Bennigan came up behind him.

He glanced over his shoulder. "Who is it?" Reporters hadn't found him here in Alpine yet, but it was only a matter of time before a reporter weaseled the information out of someone back in Cascade or from the rodeo.

"Some woman."

His heart jolted. Lavender?

"She addressed you as Mr. Craig. I didn't get her name."

He turned and stopped himself from chiding her, reminding her that her job was to find out, but he didn't have the energy for a confrontation. Instead, he moved past her and picked up the phone, hoping to hear Lavender's voice.

And being disappointed.

"Mr. Craig," Gertrude Cates said stiffly. "What do you mean leaving my girl here to deal with this on her own?"

"Deal with what?"

"Are you kidding? Do you think those reporters left when you did?"

He rubbed his hand over his forehead, perplexed. "What are you talking about?"

"They're offering her all kinds of money, calling at all hours– her picture was in the tabloids, nearly naked. She won't leave the house, and they've got people talking about whether or not she's a suitable teacher. All because of you!"

The last bit followed him out the door as he dropped the handset and raced for his truck and Cascade.

Lavender would have given anything for some brownies, but she was out of eggs. She bounced her keys in her palm and stood at the kitchen door, working up the nerve to walk out to her car. Why couldn't Gertrude drive, just that little bit? Lavender didn't want to face anyone, especially not hunting for comfort food. The reporters had left, but their damage was done, worse than any fallout she could have expected from her scene at the Longhorn. She didn't want to deal with the judgment of anyone who'd seen that awful picture, or heard about it. Good thing school was out and she could hide until, like Taylor had said, this would blow over.

The need for privacy outweighed the need for brownies. She tossed the keys on the counter, watched them slide into the coffee maker, then jumped when the phone rang. She scowled at the instrument on the wall and spun to leave the room, only to freeze when a low, slow drawl came over the answering machine.

"Come out, come out, wherever you are."

She snatched up the handset with unseemly haste. "Taylor?"

"Come to the window."

Her heart jolted. "You're here?" She looked out the front window and saw an unfamiliar truck, a big shiny silver job, not the battered Ford she was used to. "Where?"

"Back window."

She rushed across the kitchen to the sun porch and saw Taylor in the center of her yard, among her roses, sun shining on his hair, head tilted toward the house.

Looking for her.

"Good thing I didn't give into the urge to buy a dog," she said into the phone, then hung up before walking out onto the steps.

He tapped his phone's screen and tucked it into the front pocket of his jeans as he moved toward her. "I hear you're a celebrity around here."

She tossed her head and stepped onto the grass. "Someone had to be, since you weren't around."

The shine in his eyes dulled as he came closer. "You told me to go."

She folded her arms over her chest. "I did. So why are you back?"

"Why do you think?" He skimmed the backs of his fingers down her cheek.

"Needed some time in the spotlight?"

Now the curve of his lips flattened and he dropped his hand away. "What?"

"Or are you afraid I'll sell the details of our affair?"

Shock slackened his face and he moved back. "Are you kidding me? You don't think I trust you any more than that? Jesus, you can tell them any damn thing you want about me. I don't care. I came back for you, to be with you. Can't you trust me even that much?"

Chastened, Lavender backed away, stumbled on the step. She'd been so happy to see him, yet the first thing she'd done was attack him?

Of course. Hadn't she chased her mother away with the

same behavior? Did she want him to go, or was she just testing him?

Whichever, it wasn't fair to him, but now that she'd lashed out, she didn't know how to draw the words back. She didn't know how to get him to touch her again, to look at her with that shine in his eyes, with that crooked smile.

She didn't know how to earn it. But she had to try.

"You—came back for me?" She hated the shyness, the uncertainty in her own voice.

"Yes, damn it. I love you and I hate being away from you."

This time when she stumbled, she sat down, hard, on the step behind her and stared at him. "What? What did you say?"

With an exasperated roll of his eyes, he braced his hands on his hips. "I said—"

She reached up, grabbed the front of his shirt and yanked him down on the step beside her, wincing just a little when she felt the fabric give beneath her nails. "I know what you said. So... What does that mean?"

"I don't know what it means." He swept both hands through his hair, shoving it back before looking. "I know I've missed you, that I wished you were with me, that I think about you all the time. And I know you can't be with me because of your grandmother."

Those words sucked the breath out of her.

"But I can be with you. Here, or in Alpine. I can be with you wherever you need me to be. Whatever you need me to be."

She shook her head. "Why? Why would you do that? You love traveling, you love going places. Why would you stop that because of me?"

"Because all those years I was looking for home. With you, no matter where we decide it is, I'll have found it."

Everything in her went tight. Would he stay? Could she

believe he would? What had he asked her to do? Trust him. When had she trusted anyone?

When had anyone come back to take care of her?

"Are you sure?" she managed, her hand hovering over his where it rested on his jean-clad thigh.

"That depends." He pulled his hand away and looped it over her shoulders. "Is there something you'd like to say?"

Questions flew through her mind before three words crystallized there. "I love you, Taylor Craig. Or Creighton. Or whoever you are."

He turned her face to him, his palm resting on her jaw as he looked into her eyes, those gray eyes seeking the truth, softening when he found it. He kissed her softly, deeply, drawing her closer, until the telltale sound of a camera shutter echoed across the quiet lawn.

Taylor drew back, face tense as he scanned the garden for the offender, who had fled.

"How long will this go on?" Lavender demanded.

He stood and grabbed her hand, his grasp firm and strong. "Until we take the bull by the horns."

Epilogue

"COME ON, COME ON!" Taylor clapped, the sound echoing off the saltillo tiles of the open living room. He headed toward the low leather couch where Gertrude was already settled, but he kept his attention on the archway that led to the kitchen. "Two minutes 'til show time."

The beeping of a microwave was his response, and then Lavender appeared, a big bowl of popcorn in her hands. Behind her, Mrs. Bennigan carried a tray of sodas.

Lavender stopped short when her attention landed on the big screen TV, causing Mrs. Bennigan to stutter to a halt behind her.

"I don't think I can do this," Lavender said as Mrs. Bennigan righted the spilled ice and veered around her.

"The hard part's over." Taylor reached for her hand and drew her into the room, maneuvering her between him and her grandmother.

"No, it's not. Watching myself is the hardest part."

"Cover your eyes, then."

"Then I'll hear myself."

"Are you kidding? You hardly said a word."

"Be quiet," Gertrude snapped as the television announcer introduced the latest edition of *Celebrities Tonight, Where Are They Now?*

Lavender squealed and covered her eyes when a picture of she and Taylor, smiling, laughing, sitting together on the interview couch, flashed on the screen. Taylor chuckled at her reaction and mimicked the pose, sliding his arm around her shoulders and dipping his head to touch hers.

The interviewer, Evan Zander, told the viewers about Taylor's years of celebrity, then eased into his rodeo career, showing footage of him riding Angelina at the Cascade Rodeo.

"There he met the woman who would become his wife," Evan announced as the image returned to Taylor and Lavender sitting on the couch. "You married a kindergarten teacher, Taylor, and the rumor is she didn't even know who you were?"

"No," Taylor laughed from the TV.

"You didn't see fit to enlighten her?"

"I wanted her to fall in love with me, not some poster boy."

"And she did."

On the screen, Taylor grinned at Lavender. "She did."

"Lavender, how did he propose to you?"

Lavender blushed to the roots of her hair. Taylor rubbed his hand over her back encouragingly and she leaned toward Evan. "Well, his horse does these tricks, you know? He got her to spell it out in the sawdust on the rodeo floor."

"And you could read it?"

Lavender sat back with a smile and tucked her arm through Taylor's. "It was surprisingly neat."

"The two married in Lavender's hometown of Cascade, Texas." A video of their reception in the town square played on the screen. "And now they live on Taylor's Big Bend ranch, where Taylor continues training horses and steer wrestling in local rodeos. Lavender accompanies him when she can, and they cap off successful rides with a dance at the local honky-tonk."

Beside him on the couch in their living room, Taylor saw Lavender peek over her hand as she watched the two of them dance across the screen, Taylor whipping her in circles and Lavender not missing a step. She made a sound of admiration and he grinned.

"Those dance lessons paid off," she murmured. "I need to thank Samantha next time we're in town."

He opened his mouth to say something and she shushed him as Evan came back on screen, alone, addressing the audience. Taylor frowned, but she jabbed her finger at the television.

"Just prior to airing, we received an update on Taylor and Lavender. They are expecting their first child next spring."

Gertrude squealed, a girly sound, and Taylor's ears buzzed, those words spinning around and around in his head as he pushed Lavender away. He stared at his wife, whose cheeks were pink, eyes bright with happiness.

"You're-" His hand hovered over her belly.

"Uh-huh." She nodded and pressed his hand down, holding it against her. "Twins."

About the Author

MJ Fredrick wanted to be a writer from the time she was nine years old. Now she's the author of over 40 romance novels and novellas, ranging from contemporary romance to romantic suspense to historical to paranormal. She's married to her high school sweetheart for over thirty five years.

Once she graduated college with her teaching degree, she started taking writing classes, and joined the local romance writing group.

Twelve years later, she sold her first book, and a month after that, her second book, all while teaching elementary school.

Now she has moved to writing full-time after 30 years in the classroom, but she has plenty of ideas to keep her busy!

Also by MJ Fredrick

The Hopefuls Series

Hearts on Ice

Hearts on the Mountain

Starfish Shores Series

Flip-Flops and Mistletoe

Between the Rainbows and the Rain

Hearts of Broken Wheel Series

Lone Star Longing

Tumbleweed Temptation

Huisache Whispers

Ocotillo Kisses

Wild Texas Wind

Cascada Encantada Series

Perfectly Paired

A Taste of Trouble

A Rogue's Reserve

Lost in a Boom Town Series

Waltz Back to Texas

That Wild Texas Swing

Two Step Temptation

The Cowboy's Promenade

Circle on Home

Midnight Sun

A Ghostly Charm

Guarded Hearts

Eden's Promise